A GAME CALLED QUEST

S.J. LARSSON

SEVERED PRESS
HOBART TASMANIA

A GAME CALLED QUEST

ISBN: 978-1-925711-71-4

CHAPTER 1

Donny peeked up over his sister Amanda's shoulder. Yes, it was definitely Brian, Duff, and Ernie at the back of the line snaking away from Copps' front doors. He ducked out of view before they saw him.

"What is wrong with you?" Amanda asked him, rolling her eyes away from her hand mirror. Then she was back to examining her bleached hair's dark roots, not expecting an answer. Donny didn't plan on giving her one either. She'd tell him to "beat the ever-living crap out of those goons" like she did about everybody. To Amanda, anyone who wasn't punk as hell was a goon or an idiot. Donny had been called a goon at least four times a day for stupid things like dropping his Rubik's Cube or making her wait three minutes outside of the arcade at the mall when it was her designated time to meet and go. She hated being his chauffeur most of all, especially today. Donny insisted they be in line at Copps Department Store at least as early as 6 a.m. so that Donny could have a chance of picking up Pac-Man when the store opened. Copps would only have 40 copies, he explained. There would be a line a mile long.

Their mother had a house to clean on Lookout Mountain early, and she couldn't take Donny, so Donny begged and begged Amanda.

The only way he could get her to do it was by promising he'd give her his allowance for three weeks.

Luckily, their mother was more compassionate and simply gave him the thirty-five dollars he needed to buy the cherished Pac-Man. It was March 16th, 1982, a day Donny had been waiting for since he found out Pac-Man would be released for the Atari. His sister's bitchy mood wasn't going to spoil it for him. He needed this game. Needed it!

Donny leaned to the side to look for the thugs again. Now there was no sign of them at the end of the long, long line of kids and parents. Good. Maybe they realized they couldn't possibly get their grimy hands on a copy of Pac-Man, being last in line, and left. At least that's what he hoped.

"Why the hell do you keep looking back there? Think you'll get stomped? Come on. Cut it out, goon." Amanda put her mirror away. "While you're getting the game, I'm going to see if they have any of that bleach I read about in Killer's Playboy."

Killer was the drummer in the band Amanda played bass in. Amanda was eternally trying to get her chin-length hair completely white with a bluish tint. Donny knew there would be no such bleach at Copps. White hair with a blue tint had to be done at a salon. Their mother had told them that. Amanda had complained that Donny got thirty-five dollars for Pac-Man, but she didn't even get a visit to the hair salon to make her dream come true.

"You'll want your hair to be rainbow a week after you get it done," their mother had told her. "Both of you can play Pac-Man. Amanda, you have a car at least. Now. Stop your fussin'."

"Okay, good luck," he told Amanda, and looked to the front of the line. His classmate Kevin was second in line, but he was alone. No parents. Donny didn't think Kevin had any brothers or sisters. The short, fat kid with red hair and freckles skulking against the wall was barely visible with all the people. He wore the dorkiest knock-off Alligator shirt with green and blue stripes, bold colors, but they were nothing compared to his flaming hair. Donny wondered when his sister would want that color hair.

2

"You don't have to sound like such a goddamn brat all the time, Donny. God."

If their mother heard her talk like that, Amanda wouldn't have a car for a month. Donny thought about saying so, but he was in too good of a mood to bring it up.

Kevin leaned forward and saw Donny. Grinned. His braces gleamed like silver beacons in the morning sun. Donny ducked back after a short nod. He hoped nobody in line from school saw that and thought he and Kevin were friends. Talk about dorks. Donny wasn't a dork, no. Absolutely not. He might not have fifty million friends like his punk rock, worshipped sister, but he wasn't a dork.

He was just a fourteen-year-old freshman trying to keep his head down and staying out of trouble.

He felt a jab on his shoulder. Hard. He turned to his right.

Brian, Duff, and Ernie stood next to them on the sidewalk. "Hey, Donny," Brian said casually. "What's going on? Hey, you got room for us in front of you?"

"Get the hell out of here, idiots," Amanda said to them, waving her green-tipped fingers in their faces. "We got here at six. If you wanted to be in front of us, you shoulda got here at 5:55. Now, blow it out your ass, freaks."

Duff laughed, but Brian's face turned red and he frowned, looking down at Amanda. Why did she have to be so short? And Donny was an inch shorter than her. His stomach tightened, and he put his hands behind his back to hide their shaking.

"You're the freak," Brian muttered, glaring at her. "Look at your damn hair. What the hell are you trying to do to your hair, melt it?"

Ernie and Duff cackled.

"Shut the hell up or I'll tell that cop at the door you're fifteen and drove here without a license." Amanda arched an eyebrow at Brian and pointed to the back of the line. "Don't make me pull out my switchblade," she hissed.

Brian huffed, then smiled at her. "Your band sucks," he said and turned away, walking back to the end of the line. His cohorts followed.

"God," Amanda said. "They need an ass-kicking. Stupid sophomores." She had her hand in her front pocket, probably feeling so tough as she situated her switchblade.

Amanda thought that, because she was a senior, she was above all the crap. Maybe she was, but Donny wasn't sure whether or not Brian would sock it to a girl. Donny bet he would.

And then the doors flew open and everybody in line dashed madly inside. All respect for the line and rules went out of everyone's heads as they crammed through Copps' double doors.

"Angel is a Centerfold" played over the store's ceiling speakers as the horde took over Copps.

Donny lost Amanda as soon as he was in, but he didn't care. His mind was on the Atari game aisle and how to get there fastest. He weaved through kids and parents, got knocked over twice, and finally reached the precious games. He pushed through the fifty thousand or so kids scrambling to get a copy of Atari's Pac-Man, but as he got to the front, the crowd loosened up. His heart sunk. That wasn't good. As he got through to the shelf where Pac-Man should be, he almost cried. Not one Pac-Man one was left. They'd all been taken.

He heard a couple of little kids crying in the crowd, but he turned away and wandered off. Dammit, he thought. He wanted it so bad. He thought for sure by being near the front of the line, he'd get a copy. It was a nightmare. How did this happen? How did all these kids get there before him? Did someone buy a whole bunch of copies?

He dragged his feet through the toy section. He guessed he should find Amanda in the hair supplies aisle and go home. He couldn't believe it. Just couldn't believe his rotten luck. All the waiting, all the planning. He'd even gone to Copps a week before with his mother to make sure he had a firm knowledge of the layout of the store so he could get there fastest, ensure he got a copy. All his planning had come to nothing. He'd be stuck with the three crappy games he had until more Pac-Mans were delivered to the store. Yeah, he'd play the ones he had, but he wouldn't be happy about it. He'd beaten all three at least six dozen times.

"Psst. Hey, Don."

Donny looked to his right as he passed the Barbie aisle. Who was whispering his name like that?

Kevin stood next to hanging blonde Barbies with his back to Donny, looking over his shoulder at him. He had a hand cupped over his mouth as though trying to make his whisper directional.

Donny stopped and stared.

"Come here. Come here, man."

Donny didn't want to be seen with Kevin. If Brian and company came up on him with Kevin, who got it even worse than he did from the bullies, they'd both get foot stomped until their toes broke. Donny would never hear the end of it.

"Okay, look, then," whispered Kevin, and he stuck a corner of a video game box over his shoulder. *Pac-Man*, the top read. Kevin completely turned away and waited. And, of course, Donny couldn't help himself. Kevin had one. Why was he calling Donny to him in the Barbie aisle?

Donny went down the aisle to Kevin, stopping right behind him. "So, you got one?"

Kevin turned around and looked up at him. He held Pac-Man's box close to his chest with both arms covering it. "Yeah," he whispered. "Yeah, I sure as shit did, Don."

"Don't call me Don."

"Look." He unfolded his arms and displayed the glorious box.

"Good for you." It pissed Donny off. It was like Kevin was bragging. What a dweeb.

"No, wait, don't go."

Donny turned back to him. "What?"

Kevin's green eyes got round and worried. "You see, the thing is, well, I walked here."

"So?"

"You see, yeah. I walked here, and I don't got no money."

Donny blinked. "How are you going to pay for it?"

Kevin looked at his two-year-old beat-up tennis shoes. They seemed too small for him, with one big toe nail poking the sneaker's plastic tip up. "I wasn't."

"You mean, you're stealing it?"

Kevin put one hand over his mouth. "Shhh!"

Donny lowered his voice. "I don't give a crap. See ya, Kevin."

"No, no, wait. Here." He held Pac-Man out to Donny.

"What are you doing?"

"Yeah, I was gonna steal it. I ain't got no money. But I'm not gonna. I'm gonna give it to you, 'cause you'll pay for it, right?"

Donny stared at him, then the game, then back at him. "You're giving it to me," he said sarcastically.

"I ain't no thief. I thought I could, but I can't, I just can't. Ma would whip me, not that she'd notice it. But she prolly would. I mean, I think so. It's not worth the risk. I know you'll pay for it. You ain't got one." Kevin pointed at Donny's empty hands.

"Thanks for reminding me."

"Come on, take it. And maybe you can invite me over to play sometime? Maybe?" His fat cheeks got red and his eyes were desperate.

Donny sighed. He couldn't let Kevin steal it, and man, he wanted that game. He wanted it bad. Having Kevin over for a day or two to play it wouldn't be a big deal. As long as nobody found out about it.

"Okay, okay. I'll get it. Uh, thanks." He took Pac-Man from Kevin. It felt like gold in his hands. The box itself looked exciting. Was Donny really going to play his favorite arcade game right in his own house? This was happening, right after he'd just accepted it wasn't going to?

"Can I come home with you now? Yeah?" Kevin asked.

Donny didn't want him to, not today. "Maybe tomorrow."

"I ain't got a way home."

"Where do you live? You said you walked."

"I walked for an hour, man."

"My sister can drop you off."

"Then why can't she take me to your house and we can play together? Come on. I gave you the game."

"You said you got too scared to steal it."

"I was. I am. But I gave it to you. To you."

Donny sighed. "O-okay. I guess let's pay for it and wait for my sister outside."

Kevin seemed to grow an inch, shoulders back and green eyes glowing with thrill. "Thanks! Thank you so, so much, man. You're the best. I knew you'd let me play it with you. You're the absolute best."

Donny turned away from him and ran smack into Brian. Bam. Face in his chest.

"What you got there, Donny?" Brian stood a head taller than Donny and a head and a half taller than Kevin. Donny heard Kevin gasp behind him.

Duff and Ernie came out from the aisle ends and entered the Barbie aisle. "You knew we'd get your place in line somehow," Duff said in his cracking voice. He was even taller than Brian, but scrawny. Still, Donny had gotten a shiner from him before.

"Cut the shit," Kevin said, but his voice shook. "Leave Don alone and get the hell outta here, right?"

Brian didn't take his eyes off Donny. "Ernie?"

Ernie stepped around Donny and put Kevin in a headlock while giving him a noogie on top of his head with his middle knuckle. Kevin couldn't make a sound; his windpipe was blocked.

"Cut it out!" Donny said.

"Give me the game and he will," Brian said.

Donny held the game to his stomach. "No way."

Kevin made gurgling noises.

"Alright, I asked nicely." Brian hauled back and punched Donny right above where the game box covered his belly. The wind knocked out of him and he doubled over, dropping the game.

Duff swept down and grabbed Pac-Man off the floor. "Thanks, dumbass," said Duff.

Donny fell to the ground, trying to catch his breath. He looked up at the three of them. Ernie had released Kevin. They gave each other high fives.

"You girls have fun sucking each other's fat ones," Brian said. "And thanks for the game. You're the best, right?"

Duff leaned over Donny and spit a squishy loogy in Donny's short, brown hair. Some of the spray got in his eyes.

"What the hell is going on?"

In his pain, Donny couldn't see Amanda, but he recognized her voice. She must have come looking for him and had seen what happened. "Donny, you all right? Donny?" He felt her hand on his shoulder.

"Come on, let's get out of here," Duff said, laughing with the others.

"See ya, bitch queen," Brian called back to Amanda as the three ran off, sneakers squeaking on the store floor.

Amanda was bent over Donny with a tissue from her purse, wiping the spit off his face and out of his hair. "Are you okay? What was all that about? Godammit, those freaking goons!" She whipped her head around and Donny knew she wanted to go after them, but was showing unheard of concern for him. She never cared at all about him, but she looked pissed.

Donny caught his breath and sat up. "Don't worry about it."

"They took our game," Kevin said, also getting his breathing under control.

"You mean, you had the game and those freaks took it? Punched you and took it?"

"Uh, yeah."

"I'll kill them! I got up at five in the morning for this shit? What are their names? I'll get them good."

That would be the worst thing his sister could do. If she got them in trouble for beating Donny up, then he'd really get a beat-down once the trio was free of whatever punishment dealt out to them. "No, it's okay. Just forget it."

Amanda stared hard at him.

"Really." Donny sat up. Kevin offered him his hand.

"Come on, stand up."

Donny took Kevin's offering and rose to his feet, looking at Amanda.

"Well, dammit. Now what? Shit, I didn't even find that damn hair dye."

"Let's just go," Donny said.

Amanda's hard features softened. "Tell you what. I'll drive you downtown. You can spend that thirty-five on something down there by the choo-choo. Has to be something cool. Come on, I'll drop you off. Hell, I'll go with you. I play shows down there. I know some cool shops. Come on."

*

Amanda took them to a shifty area near the Chattanooga Choo-Choo downtown where most of the buildings were run-down, and there were a lot of bars and little groceries. They walked the narrow, broken streets in silence, all in bad moods. Amanda might have had the intention of cheering Donny up after he got his ass kicked, but now she acted bored.

"Look at that place. Hey, Don. Look at that place," Kevin said, pointing to a glass door covered in sixties stickers. The shop was crammed between a bar and a corner shop and had to be six feet wide.

"Never noticed that place before," Amanda said.

"I wanna go in there. Can we go in there?" Kevin asked.

"I'm not your mommy," Amanda said.

"Don?"

"Okay, sure." Donny thought the place looked kind of cool, too. The sign above the door said "Shop Royee" on a piece of cardboard, written in black marker. He peered through the murky glass before opening the door. The place looked full of knick-knacks from decades ago, shelf after shelf of junk nobody would want.

Amanda did the same. "How the hell does this place stay in business? It's a bunch of trash."

Kevin yanked the metal handle on the door and went in. Donny and Amanda followed.

Inside, there was no light except that coming in from outside. The back of the narrow shop couldn't be seen in the darkness. Nobody was inside.

"Look at this stuff!" Kevin said, picking through a shelf of weird electronics and glass valves. "What are these things?"

"I dunno, but don't touch. Some of these places down here will send you to the cops if you even look at their stuff funny," Amanda told him.

Donny went to a small table beside the shelf Kevin dug through. He saw tons of ancient books. He opened one. The writing looked Arabic. Something like that. It had pictures of dragons, all kinds and colors of dragons. "Look at these," he said to nobody, and no one looked.

"Ah, I see you've taken an interest in *Lowean Dragon Lore*. It's also a particular favorite of mine," said a man's voice from the darkness beyond. All three of their heads snapped to that direction as a man in his seventies walked into the dusty light. He had long, thinning silver hair down around his shoulders and an equally long beard. He wore what looked like a brown bathrobe and had pink bunny slippers on his feet. One of the bunny ears was chewed off on his left foot's slipper.

"Who are you?" Amanda asked, aggressive as always.

"I'm the owner, yes. I'm Royee and this is my little piece of heaven. I am the collector. Yes, I am. I collect all kinds of things. I buy, too, in case you're interested in selling me a nice thing." His voice was younger than his lined face. His eyes were black sparks deep set in his bony face.

"When did you open? I know every place on this street," Amanda said, suspicion in her voice.

"I've been here, always been here. Always will be. You must have just missed me. Hard to see, yes. Hard to see, especially at night. Especially if you don't *look*." He opened his folded hands and revealed a burning tealight in his right palm. The lines on his face grew deeper from the flickering shadows the tealight cast.

"That's just weird," said Amanda.

"Hey, dude, you got any games?" Kevin asked him, seemingly unaware of how odd the shopkeep was.

"I have plenty. Plenty of games. Board games, card games, and I have several of those hula hoops the kids go nuts for."

"Hula hoops? Are you kidding?" Amanda said.

"Got any video games?" Kevin asked.

Royee eyed him carefully then looked at Donny. "Are you video game players?"

Donny nodded because the strange man kept waiting for a response, staring at him with an innocuous expression. "Uh, yeah. I play arcade games, and I have an Atari. So, yeah. If you have Atari games… Uh, yeah." Royee made Donny nervous *because* he was odd. Who runs a shop with a tealight as the only lighting?

"Atari? People still play those things?"

The three kids looked at each other. Amanda shrugged.

"I play Atari all day and night," Kevin explained to him. "Everybody does."

Royee's black eyes widened. "Ahhhh, yes. Of course, they do. You know what? I just might have an Atari game lying around in the back. I have to find it. I made it myself."

"You made an Atari game?" Donny asked, not sure if this guy knew what an Atari was.

"I certainly did, and I made it better than all the Atari games ever made. You better believe it." He grinned, showing a gap between his front teeth. "Let me see, I'll find it. I like you three. I might give you a discount."

He turned and went to the dark back of the narrow shop, taking the tealight with him.

"He's gonna burn his hand," Kevin said.

"He didn't make a damn Atari game. Let's get the hell out of here," said Amanda.

"Wait," Donny said. "I want to see what he comes back with."

"You do?" Kevin asked.

Donny nodded, peering into the dark until he saw a small light coming back their way. When Royee came to the front where the three waited, Donny saw that Royee seemed covered, head to toe, in wires.

"You, young girl, you look like you could handle this. Yes, I think you could. You see, you plug this…into this…and then this…" He fumbled with wires, goggles, headphones, a microphone and weird-looking cable ports. "I can tell about people. I suspect you can make this brilliant contraption I made work with your Atari."

He plopped it all down on the table of books by Donny.

"What is all that?" Donny asked.

"Oh, just stuff. Stuff to make the game more enjoyable. I only have this one. It was an experiment of mine from… some time ago. See?" Royee held up a pair of thick goggles. "I brought three pairs so you could all play at the same time."

"It just looks like a bunch of cables and stuff," said Kevin, picking up a pair of old, cheap headphones. "What are these for?"

"To hear the game, young man. To hear the sounds of the game."

"I don't see no game," Kevin replied.

"That's because it's in my pocket." Royee reached into the front pocket of his bathrobe and pulled out an Atari game box. "See? It's called Quest."

Donny read the word *Quest* written on the maroon, beat-up box. There was a picture of a warrior, very much fantasy, and Donny noticed it bragged a "3D Controller."

"What is it? What's a 3D controller?" Donny asked.

"That sounds kinda cool," said Kevin. "3D controller."

"There're dragons. You like dragons. You were looking at my dragon book. Some of the dragons in that book are in this game." He grinned again. "These," he gestured over the wires and gadgets, "are the 3D controllers. You three would have absolutely the best time of your young lives playing my game."

"I don't know what to do with all this," Amanda said. "Why in the world would you think I could do something with a bunch of cables? Are there even any Atari ports on these? What the hell are the goggles for?"

"Well, you have a tongue on you. As a teenager should. Yes, there should be Atari ports somewhere in there. You have to kind of link everything up... yes, untangle and link. You'll figure it out." He rubbed his hands together after putting the game, Quest, on top of the jumble of stuff on the book table.

"Dragons?" Kevin asked. "Is this game some kind of bad D&D rip-off?"

"No," Royee said, raising his fuzzy eyebrows. "It's a very good one."

"So you say," Amanda replied. "You made it, of course you'd say that."

Royee rubbed his bony hands together after setting the tealight next to the pile of cables, headphones and goggles. "I can tell you want it," he said to Donny. "It's forty dollars. I cut you a deal."

Donny glanced at Kevin and Amanda. "I don't have forty. I only have thirty-five."

Royee frowned. "Oh, that is a problem. I require forty dollars for Quest. Now, if you perhaps have something you can trade to make up the difference, something I can sell for a profit, then yes, yes. We'd have a deal."

Donny shrugged. He was so very curious about this game, especially if there were dragons in it. He knew if there was a way to get it working on the Atari, Amanda would be able to figure it out. She'd built the bass she used, by God. "I don't have anything."

"Well, I'm sorry. I can't offer the game unless you pay the fee." Royee's face was impassive.

"Wait," Kevin said. He turned to Donny. "Will ya let me play it with you? Please? I might have something. Come on."

Donny didn't want to bring Kevin back to his house, but then again, Kevin had tried to stand up for him to Brian and his gang. That took balls. "Yeah. Yeah, I guess so. But not too late."

Kevin grinned, braces twinkling in the candlelight. "Mr. Royee, I have with me a state-of-the-art 1981 calculator. Very few of its kind were made." He pulled an everyday calculator out of his front pants pocket. It had less than four or five functions. "See? See how it calculates everything? You could easily resell this for maybe forty bucks itself."

Royee took Kevin's calculator and pressed some buttons. "Quaint. How quaint. You know, I do think I can resell this to the right buyer. Yes, I certainly could." He looked up at the three kids. "You have a deal. Now, scoop all this up. You're wasting time. And don't forget to give me the thirty-five."

Donny got the cash out of his pocket and handed it to Royee. "What do you mean by we're wasting time?"

"This is only a rental. You have to bring it back in five days."

"Now, wait a goddamn minute," Amanda said, stomping her foot. "You're ripping my little brother off."

"No, no. I promise you I'm not. I'm not ripping anyone off. You'll see, miss. The deal is done. I have the cash and the calculator. Now, you three get all this together and run, run, run home. Miss, you put it together to work. These goggles. These headphones. Yes. Here's an Atari port. There's another one in here. Now, go. Shoo! Shoo! We have a deal. If you don't return it, there will be a high fee each day it's late. But you don't want that. Trust me. In five days, you'll finish and be ready to return it. Maybe I'll even have another game for you. A game like Pac-Man? I hear that's the rage."

"Are you saying you'll have Pac-Man in this shop in five days?" Donny asked, full of disbelief.

"I did say something like that. Could be, could be. Time's long here. Now, now. Scoop, scoop, and run home. Go on. Have fun, and bless the dragons!"

"No way, Methuselah," Amanda said. "You're not ripping my brother off like that."

Donny turned to his sister. He wanted this game. He needed this game. It would keep him busy for five days until they could come back for Pac-Man. Copps wouldn't have more Pac-Mans in for weeks, maybe months. "No, it's okay, Amanda. Let's do it." He turned to Royee. "Since it's a rental, will Pac-Man be paid for?"

The strange man scratched his neck in thought with both hands. "As long as I get to keep this calculator. I already have a buyer in mind."

"Kevin?" Donny asked him.

Kevin shrugged. "If you let me play Quest. And Pac-Man."

Donny nodded and turned back to Royee. "Okay, deal."

"Idiots," Amanda muttered.

CHAPTER 2

"I hope you appreciate me. All this crap is ridiculous. Of course, I'm going to check it out after spending two and a half hours putting it all together. I'm curious now, but I'll be shocked if it works. I think you got swindled." Amanda finished duct-taping a couple spliced wires to one of the two Atari input cables. She had explained that the Atari only had two input ports in the back, and the shopkeep Royee had given them three pairs of black, opaque, thick foam-outlined goggles and three pairs of headphones. "We only have two joysticks, so I'll be a voyeur." She folded the stray end of tape on the roll over itself and tossed it to the side of the basement floor.

Their house wasn't big, but the basement filled the length and width of the upper level. When their dad had been around, he never let them come down here. It was his room, his space, and he rarely left it when home. Donny didn't miss the man who divorced his mother when he was eight. He didn't remember much about him, to be honest. Amanda said he was a cheating ass who thought with his chub, and that they all were much better without him. The only thing that bothered Donny about it was how his mother had to work every day, all day to make ends meet, as she was the only one raising them.

This basement was a game room now. Amanda didn't spend as much time here as Donny, but she would sometimes play the Atari when Donny wasn't hogging it. She also built stuff down here in a fever, and the far, back corner had a workbench and tools set up. Mostly she worked on musical instruments. Weird hobby for a girl.

Donny dug around in his game closet and found another joystick, which made Amanda have to work longer and harder.

Kevin sat impatiently smack-dab in front of the TV fiddling with his joystick, asking all kinds of questions, but most frequently, "How much longer?"

"Okay," Amanda said after plugging two fire hazard-looking jacks into the back of the Atari. "Here. You and you." She handed Donny and Kevin each a pair of goggles and headphones. "I figure this microphone just kind of sits in the middle of the room? I don't know. There aren't any instructions. Put those on and I'll turn the Atari on. Put the game in."

"But what if you miss something?" Donny asked.

"In those black goggles? I won't even see my eyeballs' reflections."

"Just put them on as soon as you put the cartridge in, okay?" Donny said.

"Fine. Go ahead."

Donny put the goggles on and couldn't see anything at all, not even a hint of light at the edges. He lifted the headphones over his ears and waited.

"Did you do it?" Kevin asked. "So, we don't even use the TV?"

"Calm down, idiot. I'm getting my stuff on. Had to make sure neither of you messed up my handiwork when you put these contraptions on. Okay, okay. Here we go. Popping it in and...now my goggles and headphones are on."

Nothing happened.

"Dammit," said Amanda. "I'm pretty sure I did everything right. The best with what I had to work with."

"Wait," Donny whispered. He thought he saw something. A glimmer of light, like a flickering flame. It had been just ahead of him in the goggle-induced night.

Nothing happened.

And then, Donny saw the flickering light again. "Hey, do you see it? The light?"

A pause, and then Kevin said, "Yeah, I see it. It looks like a fire or something. A fire? Should we go to it?"

"Go to it? How the hell do we do that?" Amanda said.

Donny pushed the button on his joystick, nothing, and then pushed forward.

"Hey!" Kevin yelled. "I see you, Don, ahead of me. You're a cartoon! You're walking in front of me. Amanda? You see that?"

Amanda was quiet, too quiet. "Yes," she finally murmured. "I see it. I see my little brother walking in front of me. Of us?"

"I can see you, too, Amanda!" Kevin cried out.

"Can you keep it down?" Amanda hissed. "We have neighbors."

"Do you see me?"

"Yes, I see you."

"What is this game? It has to be the best Atari game ever made. The best *game* game ever made." Kevin's words tumbled over each other.

"Push forward on the joystick," Donny called back to them. He was about to go around the bend of what looked like a cave path, and hoped he'd find the source of the light.

He wasn't disappointed.

Blocking any progress further through the cave stood a cloaked and hooded figure with his face hidden. He heard Amanda and Kevin reach him and stand on either side of him.

The cloaked figure's head turned as though he could see them one by one in the dark. He held a wooden torch with a weak orange and yellow flame. At his feet was a large red velvet bag.

"What do we do?" Kevin whispered. "We gotta do something. This is called Quest. We gotta get a quest. Right?"

Donny took a step toward the mysterious figure. "Hello." He felt stupid talking out loud to a game, but had to try it. "I'm Donny. Who are you?"

The figure tilted his head at him.

"This is my sister, Amanda, and Kevin. We're here to, uh, go on a quest?"

The figured nodded. In a smooth, clear voice, he said, "I am Howlinowa. I am your Game Host for Quest. Very pleased to meet you, Kevin, Amanda, and Donny. The first thing we need to address is your races and classes. Who, may I ask, is the party leader?"

"Party leader?" Amanda said. "What's he talking about?"

"It's a quest, dummy," said Kevin. "When you're on a quest, you're in a party. And when you're in a party, you have a party leader. Duh."

"Shut up."

"Don is the party leader, for sure," Kevin said, ignoring her.

The man in the cloak nodded. "You have only one race, Donny. You must be human. Now, human, you must pick your class. You can be a wizard, a warrior, or an archer."

"I want to be a warrior," Kevin blurted out. "Oh, sorry, man. If you want to. I mean, you're the party leader."

"No, it's okay. You go ahead."

"I kind of want to be an archer," Amanda said. "Donny, do you mind being the wizard?"

Donny smiled. "Not at all." It was what he would have picked, anyway.

Howlinowa asked, "And what races will you be, warrior and archer? You can be Elf or you can be Dwarf."

"I'm an Elf. With white hair with a blue tint. Can you do that, old bag?" Amanda said, all attitude.

"Yes."

Silence. Donny was a little creeped out.

Kevin wasn't. "I'm a Dwarf. One hundred percent a Dwarf. Can you make me a badass Dwarf warrior?"

"I can make you a Dwarf, and I can make you a warrior, but a great fighter only you can make of yourself through your choices and experiences."

"All right," Kevin said. "Fair enough. Do it."

"I already have."

Donny looked around him at the other two.

Amanda was easily six feet tall, and her hair fell past her shoulders in white-blue waves. She had the fairest skin and little pointy Elf ears. Cartoony Amanda. She still had on her Dead Kennedys tee, though.

Kevin was fatter than before, but all muscle and meat. He had a thick, long red beard and long red braids coming from his head. He, too, wore the knock-off Alligator shirt still.

"Look at you!" Amanda said to Kevin just as he pointed at her and gasped.

"Do I look different?" Donny asked.

They looked at him in the flicker of the naked flame. "No, sorry," said Amanda.

He didn't want to be human. They got to be an Elf and a Dwarf almost for real, it seemed. He turned to Howlinowa. "Where do we get armor? Weapons?"

At least with those, Donny could somewhat look different than himself.

"Happy you asked," he said. Donny still hadn't gotten a look at the features under the hood. Howlinowa pointed at the red velvet bag. "Inside, you will find such. I assure you everything will fit and be suitable. Now, go ahead. Dress and arm yourselves. Then I will give you your stats."

"Ohhhh," Kevin said. "This *is* like D&D. This is such a cool game. Yeah."

Donny leaned over to open the bag, trying not to worry about how this game worked. It was too fun. Amazing, actually. He untied the gold drawstring…and then all three of them flashed like white stars in the narrow cave passage.

Donny opened his eyes. His sister wore a form-fitting black leather suit with brown leather straps and solid silver buckles. Strapped to her belt were a multitude of throwing knives, and strapped to her back was a giant silver-gilded black longbow. She wore a black leather sheath full of arrows, little sparks flying off the feathers.

Kevin was decked out in gold-and-red chainmail from head to toe, with a golden helmet only revealing his glowing green eyes and red, coarse beard. His helmet had long, white ox horns on either side of his head. He held a gigantic battle ax that Donny swore had a splatter of dried blood on it.

They all looked at each other, talking at once.

"What do I look like?" Donny asked.

They stopped and looked at him. "You look like you, but way cooler," said Amanda. She sounded excited. "You're wearing a royal blue robe with white fur trim, and you're covered in jewelry."

"Sparkling jewelry!" Kevin added.

Donny reached to the belt at his waist and pulled a wand out that had been stuck in the band. It was a twisted piece of birch branch with gemstones set into the wood's notches. The tip glowed a soft violet.

"Yeah, not bad. How is this even happening?" Amanda asked.

"Who cares? Howlinowa," Kevin said, turning to the Game Host. "Now what? Don't you give us the quest?"

"What quest?" the man asked calmly.

"The game is called Quest. So, you have to give us a quest. Oh, and the stats, you said. What are our stats?" Kevin rubbed his chainmail gloves together in anticipation.

"I will hereby designate your beginning stats. The stats of this world are Strength, Defense, Agility, Charm, Intellect, and Purpose. As you continue, you will find each of these stats play their part." He reached in a sleeve and pulled out three scrolls. "These are your Level 1 stats. You, you, and you." He handed each of the kids a scroll. "Look at this. Keep this. It will change as you level. Not all stats level the same for all classes. You will see. Open them and learn them."

Donny unrolled his scroll.

He would be a Level 1 Human Wizard, a character type he liked. However, his numbers for almost everything were mediocre to outright awful: Intellect, the most important for a Wizard, was just a 6, Purpose 5, Charm 4, Agility 3, Strength 2, and Defense a measly 1. It was obvious that he would have to rely on the stronger characters to keep him alive while he cast his spells.

Even as he read (he saw that he had 30 Hit Points, as well as Storm Rage and Fireball powers that worked with his Strength and Intellect), he was already committing his stats to memory.

Kevin's were a little better, even though he was a Dwarf Warrior, something Donny didn't find particularly exciting. Kevin read them out to the rest of the group: Intellect was 1 (figured, for a Dwarf, Donny thought with a smile), Charm 2, Agility and Purpose both at 4, and Strength and Defense both at 7. Hit points at 55/55 and a good mix of all the physical stats needed for a little thug. Kevin's numbers were pretty much the opposite of Donny's, which worked for what they needed to do with and for each other.

Amanda was about to share hers before Donny snatched her sheet away and read it to everyone: "What do we have here... okay, Amanda's an Elf Archer—"

"Nice," Kevin said.

"—with Strength 6, Agility 6, Defense and Purpose both 4, Charm 3, and Intellect 2. Boy, do they have *you* down," he said with a laugh, one that Amanda didn't share. "36 of 36 Hit Points, blah blah, Strength and Agility blah, regular Elf stuff."

"Let's go, already," Amanda said, taking her page and swatting Donny with it.

"Yeah, this is gonna be so cool," Kevin said.

Donny stuck his in one of his robe's many pockets. Kevin and Amanda had bags now, and put their scrolls in them.

"In order to gain Level 2, you must reach 100 experience points. You gain experience points by defeating foes. The higher level a foe is, the more experience points you will receive. In order to reach the next level, you must get one and a half experience points from the level prior. You each will receive the same experience points, and it is spread amongst the party members. This is the information I am to deliver to you."

"So," Kevin said to Howlinowa, "what about our quest?"

The cloaked man nodded, face still not showing. Donny noticed he had a rope hanging from his shoulder with miniature dangling human skulls on it. "Your first quest is to travel out of this cave and north to the Alliance city of Pariss. There, you will seek out Asope. He will give further instruction. Now, I will give you all your first moves and spells. Abilities. The ones you can use now are on your stat scrolls. More will appear as you learn them.

"Amanda, as an Elf, you have Touch of Land, Passive. You regain small amounts of HP over time. Your first fighting ability is Sharp Shot. Use it wisely, and fight from afar. Range is your greatest advantage. Your class-specific ability is Insight. When you use this, you can examine foes for their levels and stats, and then plan with your party accordingly."

He turned to Kevin. "Kevin, as a Dwarf, you have Appetite, Passive. Any food or drink items you consume for ability or stat boosts will have double the effect. Your first fighting ability is Slice. Damage your foes hard with it at opportune moments. Always protect your party. Your class-specific ability is Savior. With this, you can entice a monster to stop attacking its target and, instead, come after you."

Howlinowa turned to Donny last.

"Donny, as a human, and the only human in our land, you have Power of One, Passive. When you engage an opponent in battle with damage, you cut the opponent's Purpose stat in half over the duration of your battle. Your first fighting ability is Fireball. You do high damage, but have a weak constitution. Beware of this. Your class-specific ability is Storm Rage. With this, you cause a thunderstorm that does small amounts of damage to multiple enemies in range for over a time period of twenty seconds."

Howlinowa paused, turning his hooded head back and forth among them. "Now, your abilities are listed on your stat scrolls, and as you gain more abilities, they will also be added to your stat scrolls. I believe it is time for you to travel on. As you exit the cave, you will see a user interface overlaying your vision of this place. From it, use your joystick to select your choices, such as what ability to use. Worry not on the rest of this world's mechanics. You are here to complete an important quest for the sake of all. For the sakes of yourselves. Through your travels, the exact nature of the quest will be revealed to you."

He turned his back to them and faced the cave tunnel winding up ahead of them. "Follow this path to the surface. There are many foes between here and the Alliance city of Pariss in the North. Asope can be found in the Palace of Pariss. He is of royal blood. My new friends and adventurers, welcome to the land of Quintarria."

*

Above ground, they found themselves in a thick, dark wood full of strange sounds coming in through their headphones. Nobody asked questions. They were too excited and, well, sucked in. Kevin kept saying he couldn't wait for the first battle. Donny wished Howlinowa had followed, but the Game Host repeatedly said, "I will see you again when the time is right." At least that part was machine-like.

The graphics were insanely realistic. Way better than the absolute best arcade games. Everything looked like a cartoon, but Quintarria had depth. The high trees of the forest they surfaced in didn't move with any wind, but Donny heard what seemed like strange insects and birdsong.

They didn't even have a chance to have a conversation by the third time Kevin expressed how much he wanted to "Get a fight on." With a rustling in the leaves to their right, a green, burly Orc who appeared to be a warrior like Kevin, from his dress and mace, screeched and sprang at them.

Donny fell back on his butt.

Amanda squealed but towed back on her bow, aiming for the thing's head.

Kevin really was ready. He took control so fast that Donny didn't have time to feel stupid for thinking he was, for real, about to get sliced up with the Orc's hand ax. Ignoring the disgusting slobber coming off the thing, Kevin rushed at the Orc and jumped so that one of his Dwarf feet connected with the Orc's knee, and he used that for leverage to leap high enough to swing his ax and slice through the tendons of the monster's left arm—unfortunately, that wasn't the Orc's weapon arm, but it was good for 11 damage.

He landed on the ground behind the Orc and hissed *"Yesss!"* in triumph, but too soon: the Orc swiftly swung at Kevin and knocked him onto his leather-clad butt for 6 damage. Dwarves don't call for help, but the look on Kevin's face drove Wizard Donny into action, throwing a mad yellow fireball right into the Orc's face.

"Boom! 8 damage!" Donny cried as the creature went up in flames—but didn't fall.

Amanda stepped up with her bow and unleashed the Sharp Shot move in their foe, thunking the arrow's tip right into the Orc's already injured left arm and completely detaching it. It howled at the additional 8 damage, making all of them cover their virtual ears.

"He's still not going down! Kevin, get over here—" Before Donny could say anything more, the Orc whacked him for 6 more damage, not even using his club. Instead, he backhanded the Dwarf like a punk and took his HP from 30 to 24.

"That's not cool," Kevin yelled, wiping blood from his mouth. As the Orc now charged for Donny, Kevin assumed his Savior mode and caught the thing's attention. Donny realized Kevin was saving them, and Kevin gave them the opportunity to take their shots at the distracted Orc.

They did. Donny ran and grabbed the Orc's severed arm and enhanced it into a Magic Weapon. He pointed it like a wand and blasted a blue beam of who-knew-what right at the creature's head. At the same time, Amanda loaded up another arrow and let it fly at the Orc's chest. The attacks hit simultaneously and tore the Orc apart.

"Okay, 5 damage," Kevin said, taking stock of his injuries with an exhausted grin. "Not too bad. Not with you guys around."

They stood there, stunned at how awesome and fun the fight had been. Donny had seen the game fight text scrolling at the bottom of his game's menu. He asked the others if they had, and yes, they had.

"You guys," said Kevin. "What's your HPs at?"

"Mine is the same," Amanda said.

"I'm alright at 44HP," Kevin said, puffing up proudly.

"I got 24HP left," Donny told them. "I need better Defense."

"How do we get our HPs back?" Amanda asked. "I mean, I'll regain mine, but you two?"

"No freaking clue," said Donny. "What happens when you get to zero HP?"

"Ha, I'll never get to zero," said Kevin.

"Let's stay focused, guys," Amanda said, putting her Elven hand on her hip. She had sharp, perfect fingernails. If only she could see her hair, Donny thought. She'd be pleased to know she found the color she'd been looking for. "We have to go north to the city of Pariss and find Asope. The royal."

"Man, how do you remember this stuff?" Kevin asked her.

"Because I'm not an idiot and paid attention. Come on, let's get to Pariss. I have stuff to do when Mom gets home in a few hours."

Donny grinned at her. "It's not so bad, right?"

"You shush." She grinned and took the lead, heading what would be north in their world, judging by the sun.

On the road to Pariss, Donny stuck with Fireball mostly, with Kevin Slicing and Amanda using Insight and Sharp Shot on their foes. They fell into a comfortable pattern of slaughter as they met several other Orcs, all running solo. Most were warriors, but there were a few gunmen. Yes, they had guns. Donny thought it would take forever to level to Level 2, but by the time they breached a wooded hill and looked down on a pine valley due north with a spiraling city made of black stone ahead, they'd all reached Level 4. Every time they leveled up, they filled to full HP.

"That must be Pariss," said Amanda with a sigh. "It's dark and beautiful. I bet it's Elven."

Donny wondered how much time had passed. He didn't care. He was having too much fun. His stats scroll now had him as a Level 4 Wizard—*nice*—and his Intellect had jumped to 11! Even his Strength had soared to 6. This was good news, especially the 60 Hit Points. If it weren't for HP filling at every level-up, they'd all be screwed, except for Amanda, maybe. She knew how to dodge hits, stay out of range, and she had Regain.

*

"I think Howlinowa's creepy," said Amanda. "And just look at the walls of Pariss. There are Orcs every few feet, and they're loaded with weapons."

Donny thought, but didn't come up with anything as Kevin chattered.

"I can take them all. Just gotta do it one by one. Right, Don? Right?"

"I dunno," said Donny. "What happens in this game if our HP goes to zero?"

"I'll tell you what happens," a young male voice said from behind them. Donny spun around.

A clean-cut Elf with a bluish tint to his skin stood behind them, leaning against one of the foreboding, towering pine trees of the forest. He wore a black cape with maroon leather armor beneath. At one hip, he had a jagged dagger and the other, a wand. His light brown hair was tossed to the side, covering one pointed ear, leaving the other exposed. It bore gold hoop earrings all down the outer edge.

"Who the hell are you?" Amanda asked.

"Name's Asope."

Kevin ran at him and stopped right in front of him. "Asope! We have a quest to find you. All hail, Great Asope. I'm Kevin. I don't know why we're supposed to find you, but this guy in a robe said our quest was to find you and talk to you. You're supposed to be in a palace in Pariss. Hey. You know Howlinowa?"

"All hail?" Amanda said with a groan.

"Hey," Kevin said to her. "We're warriors. In a fantasy game. Gotta talk like it, jeez."

Asope didn't flinch at Kevin's zooming advance, but rather chuckled and grinned down at Kevin. "A Dwarf. Dwarves never come out from underground. And you," he said, eyes moving to Donny. "A human. No humans here. Not in Quintarria. How curious. No wonder Howlinowa sent you to find me."

"So? So?" Kevin continued. "We're here. We finished Howlinowa's quest to find you. Where's the loot?"

"Loot?" Asope asked with a lazy smile.

"Reward. We gotta get a reward for finishing a quest. Right? Right, Don? Amanda?" He looked around at all of them. "Sir Asope?"

"His stats are through the roof. Insight says it. He's a half-Elf, level 65, and Purpose is at 77."

"Daaaaaaamn," Kevin whooped. "Asope, you could wipe us out without even thinking about it, right? Sorry, man, didn't mean to be so pushy. Yeah, sorry... Don? You talk to him. You can figure out what's going on."

Donny examined Asope. He seemed friendly enough. "Asope, if you don't mind, uh, sir Elf. Half-Elf. What happens when our HP goes to zero?"

Asope laughed. "You die."

Silence, then Amanda said, "What happens when we die?"

"Don't worry about that. You have a plethora of Elves rooting for you." He paused, eying them, and then continued.

"You don't want to go into Pariss. The Orcs will slaughter you with your low levels and few abilities. Trust me." He stood tall and patted Kevin's armored shoulder. "Yes, I have rewards for your finding me. But really, I found you. I've been waiting around outside. Word on the wind was that adventurers had arrived to combat the control and oppression of Quintarria. That a human has come. Here, before I explain myself, let me gift you with new abilities."

Amanda stepped back. "What kind of abilities?"

He shook his head with a casual grin. "Orcs, when in groups, gain +1 Purpose for each Orc fighting together in a party. All the Orcs of Pariss are continually in a party. See? No hope for you, except maybe you, Donny the Human Wizard." He wagged a finger at Donny. "But not until you've reached a higher level. If things play out as we hope, you won't have to worry about the Orcs of Pariss."

"What exactly is Purpose?" Donny asked.

"It's what drives all races and beings. As a human, Donny, you have a special race-specific passive trait that lowers the Purpose in half against foes as you go. If you were a higher level, maybe your party would have a better chance storming Pariss, but, I think not yet. Hopefully, never."

"Who the hell are you and why don't you just tell us the next quest, give us the abilities for finding you?" Amanda demanded.

He shook his head, flowy, chin-length brown hair brushing his cheeks. "One thing at a time, fellow Elf."

"You're not an Elf. No way," said Kevin. "You're all blue. If Amanda is an Elf, you're something like an Elf, but not an Elf. But kinda. What are you, Asope?"

"I'm a half-Elf mage. I'm a third-generation child of the Vople Nole'on Alliance of Pariss. Part of the alliance agreement was that third-generation half-Elves were freed of the bonds of servitude imposed by Serranti. My great-great-grandmother was a Dark Elf, and my great-great-grandfather is an Elf. That's why I'm half-Elf."

"Serranti? Who is that?" Donny asked, suddenly quite interested. He forgot about the possibility of new abilities for the moment.

"You don't yet know of Serranti?"

They all shook their heads. "We don't know nothing, Lord Asope," said Kevin.

"Jesus," Amanda muttered.

"Will you tell us who he is?" Donny added.

Asope's cheer faded and he became solemn. "He's my great-great-great-grandfather. He rules all of Quintarria. His daughter secretly married Lale, an Elf, but she was a Dark Elf. They spawned countless half-Elves. We speculate that Serranti's only weakness, at least 2000 years ago, was his daughter, Dark Elf Merini. She and Lale hid away in Pariss, but their children, their half-Elf children, couldn't be hidden forever.

"Who knows the real story? I don't. All I know is that Serranti destroys anyone and everything in his path that he sees as an obstruction to his all-consuming power over Quintarria. As a third-generation half-Elf born from Merini and Lale, I was released from serving the Orcs and Dark Elves who occupied Pariss at my birth. It was written in the alliance. Pariss was once a thriving elven city. You can look at it, even from this distance, and see how the life has been drained from it because of Dark Elf magic and Orcish occupancy."

"I don't get it," Kevin said.

"Shut up, Kevin," said Amanda. She addressed Asope. "So, we can't go to Pariss? We can't go to the city?"

Asope raised a brown, arched eyebrow at Amanda.

"Wait," Donny said. "Just wait a minute. You said this Serranti rules over Quintarria. Why did third-generation half-Elves get the freedom you mentioned? What does that mean? Why was there an alliance in the first place? Who is Serranti, and why do you talk about Merini in past tense? Is she dead?"

Asope looked at the fallen, brown pine needles on the ground, shifted them with a sandaled foot. "Yes, yes. Serranti made the alliance, the one that said third-generation half-Elves born of Lale and Merini would be free. I have more Dark Elf in me than Elf, but that didn't manifest in my appearance. Nor, I might add, in my perceptions." He fell quiet for a moment, and then continued. "A Wizard-knight, I don't know his name, slaughtered her many, many ages ago. There are many Wizard-knight half-Elves, even more back then."

"I'm so confused. How old are you?" Donny asked.

"I'm 403 years old."

"What? How long do Elves live?" Donny asked.

"Oh, say, 6,000 years or more, depending on their class. Elves and dark Elves begin procreating around 80 years of age."

Amanda cocked her head at him. "How many Elf babies do you have?"

He chuckled and leaned back against his tree, folding his arms across his chest. "I've none."

"Why not?" Amanda pursued.

"I have not yet met my mate. According to the Vople Nole'on Alliance, I am free in Pariss, but I cannot leave. I know all in Pariss."

"Hey, you don't like Dark Elves. That's right, isn't it?" Kevin said.

Asope's expression turned more serious. "Serranti is a harsh and unjust leader. He unleashed Orcs, Trolls, and undead from underground to the lands of Quintarria. Only the Dwarves lived underground with them, but kept them in the deepest recesses of the lands. Caves, tunnels. The Orcs were the only ones sentient enough to have developed civilizations in the depths. They were who Serranti released first. The Orcs hold Pariss for Serranti."

Donny thought for a moment. "What's Serranti to you, other than a blood relative? You sound careful, like you're being overheard. Tell us, who is he and what kind of overlord is he?"

Asope stood tall and shrugged. "He controls all. He controls me. He has the Trolls holding the old Elven city of Laranda to the east, and the undead in Sillia to the south. The only city the Elves were able to keep was the stronghold of Maniunk to the west. Oh, and don't forget. While Serranti holds power over the Orcs, Trolls, and undead, he also populates the three major fallen Elven cities with Dark Elves."

"But what is the difference between Elves and Dark Elves?" Donny asked.

Asope sighed and watched Pariss for a moment as the sun dipped low in the west. "I don't want to overload you. There's so much. You should focus on the quests given to you, one at a time."

"Well, then, give us our reward for finding you and give us the next quest. Easy peasey," said Kevin. "No more questions asked." He frowned. "Well, one more. Is this Serranti a really bad guy? I mean, what's the deal with him and us?"

Asope walked toward Kevin and Donny. "You don't want to be in Serranti's path. If he hears there is a human in Quintarria, he'll go mad, doing everything he can to find him—you, Donny—and murder him. Sun's low. I'm a free man in the city, but not outside its walls. I know Stealth to get here and back. For now, you've been told enough. Little pieces at a time, my Earth friends. Here, as you asked, I will grant your quest rewards.

"Amanda, I grant you the ability Triple Shot. You may now shoot three arrows at once."

Amanda's Elven blue eyes widened. "Thank you, Asope! What a great treat." She pulled out her stat scroll and read the new ability's details.

"To you, Kevin, I grant the ability Block. You can use this to block attacks from not just you, but from anyone you choose. As many as you choose."

"Really? Really, man? Thank you!" He, too, opened his stat scroll and read.

Asope turned to Donny. "Human mage, I have a new spell to gift you for completing the quest, as well. You may now cast Cure on you or anyone you see fit. How many Hit Points you Cure for is determined by your Purpose and Intellect stats. You'll see what I mean."

"When will we see what you mean?" said Amanda.

Asope didn't answer, and instead said, "You will also find spell scrolls on fallen foes, one-time casts that will help you progress."

"Cure," Donny murmured, and also opened his stat scroll. Yep, Cure was now listed under Passive, Power of One, and his Fireball. He would be able to Cure HP damage. So, maybe they'd never find out what happened if HP reached zero. "Thanks!"

"You are most welcome. I have another quest for you. I'm sorry I cannot explain answers to the many questions you must have. It is the design of the quests that you expedite your main reason for being here, and we don't have time standing so close to Pariss. If the Dark Elves or Orcs of Pariss caught wind of a human in Quintarria, you'd all be hunted like Serranti hunted the Elves during the Elven War. But that's a story for another time. For now, I suggest you rest. You've fought hard to get here, and I'm impressed with your progress."

"Our level 4s ain't nothing compared to your level sixty thousand, sir half-Elf," said Kevin.

Asope smiled at him. "To save your progress in Quest, you must find Save Points. They are fountains spread throughout Quintarria, mostly around the four major cities. There's one you should use southwest of here. It's on the way to the Elven stronghold of Maniunk in the west. Close by. Follow this trail, this one right here. Amanda? An Elf, especially an archer, will see it. Do you see the trail?"

Amanda looked beyond Asope. "I-I—wait. Yeah. Yeah, I see a sparkling trail behind you."

"Follow it. Your new quest is to travel to the stronghold of Maniunk and find Lale. He will explain more. But first, you must save and exit, rest. Eat. And speaking of eating, I have a gift for you, Dwarf," Asope said with a smile while reaching in the pouch at his hip. "This is Pork Cheek Pie. Your Passive will like this. Eat it, and it will give you +20 Defense and +10 Strength for ten minutes. You may need it in your travels to Maniunk. Now, Amanda, lead them to the Save Point. You have your new quest. Rest and return, for there is much to do."

"Asope," Donny asked, realizing the half-Elf was doing everything to move them along. He had one last question. "Is Serranti the bad guy?"

Asope's casual demeanor and loose stance disappeared. He stiffened, stood straight, and looked Donny deep in his eyes. "You are here, Donny, human Wizard, to do everything in your power to stop Serranti and his never-ending hunger to control and oppress. Quintarria has gotten too small for him. Now he seeks expanding outward. Find Lale in Maniunk. Don't worry, we will cross paths again, probably more than a few times. I must go. I have been away from the palace too long. Serranti cannot find out there is a human in Quintarria. Rush, now, rush to the Save Point's fountain."

CHAPTER 3

"I don't understand," said Amanda. "We had to be playing that game for at least six hours. It's still daylight." She untangled headphone wires from her overdeveloped, dry hair. "Mom's not even home, Donny."

"It's only two. Two in the afternoon. We got everything running at one," said Kevin. "Is this game like real magic somehow?"

Amanda punched his arm. "Don't be stupid. It just seemed longer."

Donny scarfed his chips and gummies. "Mom won't be home until after seven tonight. We have five days. This is the weekend. When we're in school, we won't have as much time. We got five days. It's two now, so we should go back in."

"Are you a crazy person? No way. There's something messed up about playing this game. No games look like that. No games are that interactive. And, absolutely no games have a weird time difference when you're playing and then not playing the game. It's freaky," Amanda said.

"So, now you're admitting it. The time thing."

"I'm just saying. It's all too weird."

"Quit being a pussy, pussy," Kevin told her.

She punched him so hard on his upper arm that his eyes watered.

"Don't ever, *ever* call me a pussy, goon."

"Amanda, think. This is a once in a lifetime thing," said Donny. "Does this happen to anybody? No way. But it's happening to us. We gotta get back in there. Here, have some of my chips. There are a few handfuls of gummies left. Then we go back in and travel to Maniunk. Find Lale."

"I got Gobstoppers," said Kevin. "Put one in your mouth, suck on it while you play. Keep your blood sugar balanced."

"That's bullshit. It'll only give you a sugar rush," said Amanda.

"Want one?" Kevin asked, ignoring her sarcasm.

She glared at him. Donny wondered if she was about to punch his arm again.

The basement phone rang, making them all jump.

"Get it, Donny."

"You get it. I don't want to talk on the phone," Donny answered her.

"No, you get it. If you want me to even consider playing that weird-ass game again, you have to answer the phone. It might be Mom."

Donny groaned and went to the basement phone, and picked up the receiver. "Hello?" He wanted to get on with playing Quest. This was a stupid distraction.

"What you doing? Playing with your boyfriend?"

Donny's heartrate picked up. He recognized Brian's voice, and heard snickering on the line in the background. Other people in the room. Donny didn't say anything.

"Oh, the silent treatment. I've never met anyone as wimpy as you, and now, there're two of you. Donny and Kevin, sittin' in a tree. We saw him go in your house. What are you doing in there, making out? Did he give you a hickey on your nip?" More laughing from those listening to Brian. Had to be Ernie and Duff.

"Who is it, Donny?" Amanda asked.

Donny was frozen. Brian had never called his house. Donny didn't know Brian knew where he lived, but Donny knew where Brian lived. It was just a few blocks over by the neighborhood pool.

"Donny? Earth to Donny. Who is it?" Amanda asked.

He slammed down the phone. "Nobody. Wrong number."

The phone rang again. Donny refused to answer.

"Dammit, what the hell?" Amanda grunted. "Here." She shoved Donny away from the wall phone and picked it up. "You got the wrong number," she said when she answered. She listened for a few seconds. "You little pieces of shit. How did you get this number? Why the hell are you calling my house? I'm going to call the cops for harassment."

A pause.

"Oh, I sure as shit can prove it's you."

Another pause.

"That's it. I'm hanging up. If you so much as think of my little brother's name again, I'll choke you with my high bass string. It'll slice right through your neck while you're still alive. You'll bleed out your neck, mouth and ears, then you'll eat it. Now, little turd goon, hang the damn phone up and never call back."

A longer pause.

Amanda slammed the phone down. "Damn bullies."

"What they say? What they want?" Kevin asked, eyes wide and afraid.

Amanda crossed the basement to the windows near the ceiling, which would be right at ground-level on the outside. "They freaking looked in the windows and saw us with all this crap hooked up. That brat shit Brian what's-his-name and his friends want to play the game. How the hell do they know we're even playing a game? What the hell they looking in our windows for? Donny? Who are these freaks? Why are they after you to the point where they steal your Pac-Man and instead of playing it, they come stalk our basement windows?"

Donny looked at his hands.

Kevin cleared his throat.

Amanda eyed each of them curiously. "What? What did you do?"

Donny looked back up at her. "I didn't do anything. Promise. Look. It's nothing."

"Spill it or I'll... I'll tell Mom. I'll tell her to call the cops on those freaks."

Donny hesitated. Looked at Kevin, who shrugged. Everyone in his class probably knew, but Amanda was older.

Sure, he had been eight when his deadbeat dad left his mother for another woman, but what Amanda didn't know was what other woman.

"It's Brian's mom. Dad. Dad, you know. I don't know."

Amanda examined him, and then relaxed her shoulders. "It's okay, just tell me. I won't be pissed. I'm not pissed at you, it's him. It's them."

Donny sat back down on the floor in front of the TV, which hadn't even been turned on for Quest. The goggles and headphones did it all. He put his head in his hands. Amanda said she wouldn't get angry, but he knew she would.

"It's just rumors, Amanda."

Kevin cleared his throat.

"What do you know, Kevin? Spill it, one or both of you."

Kevin started to talk, but Donny cut him off. "The story in our class is that Dad left Mom for Brian's mom. They had an affair. Dad never would marry her or anything like that, and then dropped her before he moved to Texas. Brian's mom left his dad for our dad. That's just the rumor. I mean, it was, like, six or seven years ago. I don't even know if it's true, but Brian supposedly comes after me because it's my fault somehow that his mom was a cheater with Dad."

Amanda's face turned red with fury, and her brown eyes were like the daggers her archer carried in her leather belt. "What the hell has that got to do with you? Even if it is true?"

Donny looked at the shag carpet.

"I might be able to...put some perspective on this, uh..." Kevin said. Kevin never stuttered.

They both looked at him expectantly.

"Okay, so, whatever happened with moms and dads and cheating and divorces and lies, with a kid like Brian and his little crowd of Nazis, it doesn't matter what the story is. You saw him in Copps. Ernie choked me out because Brian wanted him to. My mom and dad don't know his family."

"But you were talking to me," Donny said.

"Doesn't matter, Don. Lookit. Brian's a big, fat ass. His friends are just as bad. If it weren't you and this rumor was or wasn't true, he'd find another target." Kevin sat in front of Donny. "He's a wuss deep down. If it weren't for Ernie and Duff, we could take him."

Donny wasn't so sure. Brian had been either outright beating the crap out of him, or brutally insulting and embarrassing him since he was eight. He remembered being terrorized by Brian more than he remembered his own father's face. "He's never come near the house. Amanda's right. Why was he here and looking in the basement windows when he just got Pac-Man? It makes no sense."

"Yeah, yeah it does, Don. He's a stinking, rotten person, and he has to make himself feel like the big fish because he's a mean kid who enjoys picking on you. You're an easy target. You were, what? Three feet tall when he started with you?"

Amanda sat down with them. "Is this true? Has that shit been doing this since Dad left?"

Donny stared at the carpet and nodded.

"Why the hell didn't you tell me? Or Mom? Or the school?"

"It's not a big deal."

"No," Amanda insisted. "Why didn't you tell? That's a long freaking time."

Donny met his sister's eyes. "Let's just play, okay?"

"Donny…"

"I'm not talking about this. We'll pull the blinds. Screw that guy. He can call all he wants. House is locked. What's he gonna do, throw a grenade in here?" Donny said.

Amanda tried a few more tactics to get Donny to talk, but he kept his eyes glued to the carpet and only lifted them to glance at the wires coming out of the Atari.

"Fine. Fine, fine. Okay. Be bullied. I won't dare try to help you again. If the phone rings, you answer it. If the doorbell goes off, you get the door."

Finally, Donny looked up at her. "Amanda, let's just get to Maniunk. Let's find Lale. Let's get through this mystery. That one isn't important, and I don't have answers. He's a dick. That's all there is to it. Look. Kevin just drew the blinds. It's only three now. We play the game for six hours, and less than one passes here. We have time to get to Maniunk. To fight more. To level up, learn more skills. We only have five days of this game, for crying out loud. You'll still have time to do whatever you have to do tonight that's so important. Amanda?"

Donny was somewhat shocked that Kevin kept his mouth shut through all this, especially that he had the generosity to close the basement window blinds without prompting. Donny gave Amanda one last imploring look, and finally, Amanda caved.

"All right, all right. Kevin, give me one of those Gobstoppers. A red one. Okay, let's get our gear on and see what happens when we turn the system back on. For all we know, it won't work ever again."

"Don't worry, it will," Donny told her.

"How do you know?" She still sounded irritated.

Kevin finally piped in. "Don is a Wizard. Right, Don?"

"Please, for the love of Christ, Kevin, call me Donny."

*

The snowy mountain pass that Donny, Kevin, and Amanda had to cross through to get to Maniunk was covered in little white faerie-like creatures floating just above the ground that were visible only because their silver wings reflected the moonlight. "Aw, hell," Donny said, unconsciously stopping in his tracks. "You guys ever seen Snow Imps before?"

They had not.

Amanda got that look like when she used Insight and read her game chat. "They're not hard to beat, but there's so many of them."

Donny nodded at Kevin the Dwarf, who had two axes crossed on his back. "Let Amanda use one of your weapons. Arrows are really no use against these things, but swing those axes and you should be good. Just knock down as many as you can—they're fragile and will die when they hit the ground."

"Okay," Amanda said, deferring as she accepted one of Kevin's weapons, "so they're not dangerous?"

"Oh, they're dangerous, all right. What they do is—*ow!*" Donny yelped as the first Imp that saw them dived in and took a small but bloody bite out of his arm. "*Attack!*"

Amanda and Kevin took a back-to-back position, which allowed them to pivot and strike down the offending little jerks. Two snapped pieces out of Kevin's ankles and one tore out some of Amanda's hair, but other than that, it was a silvery bloodbath on their end.

Donny didn't give the Imps a chance to get him again. He used an incantation to summon a man-sized electric ball of magic energy right where a clutch of the things were floating, cast from a scroll he found on a body, incinerating them on the spot.

Cure after hits from the Imps was Donny's main focus afterward, with Amanda Triple Shooting from interesting angles, twisting her lithe Elven body this way and that, and Kevin Blocking, Slicing, and becoming Savior at all the right times.

Donny even got to throw out Imp-ending Fireballs, which pleased him greatly. But first and foremost, he made sure everybody was Cured to the highest HP he could manage. As they went, Kevin developed creative battle cries, such as, "Dastardly Snow Imp, I vanquish you to the depths of hell and beyond!" before a Slice that seemed to do more damage than others.

When they were all destroyed, Donny laughed and said, "See? Easy-peasy."

Amanda rubbed her head where the hair had been yanked from the roots. "Yeah, swell," she said sardonically.

"Okay, yeah, not *so* fun, but look at your sheets—*Level 21, people!*" Donny smiled at his new stats, all of them now at Level 21, and his Wizard's Intellect and Purpose hitting 34, with the rest over 20, not to mention a solid 220 HP.

Kevin's total HP was 225 now, and he'd mastered his Savior move, along with Block, and only Kevin took hits for now. Donny wasn't surprised—the Dwarf had really showed his stuff against the little buggers.

And so the journey to Maniunk went on as they traveled through the Imp-infested snowy pass.

"God, I have to sit on my ass," Amanda said after another group of Snow Imps, with some special Crystal Snow Imps joining in, had been wiped out and no more were in the immediate vicinity.

"No, we gotta keep going," said Kevin. "We gotta be almost there. You'd think someone woulda given us a map, right?"

"Look at that bend up ahead. Who knows what's just around there? It curves down. Narrow." Amanda complained.

"I agree with Kevin. We gotta go," said Donny. "And we're on a roll here!"

"Come on, Amanda. Don't be a drag," Kevin told her. She shot him a look.

Donny paid no attention, keeping focused on the game. "Not bad, right?" Donny said. "It's weird how my Purpose goes up more. I don't know why. Oh, well. I'm so ready to be at Maniunk."

"We're gonna wipe out, Donny," Amanda told him. "Come on. We need to get to higher levels before going around that bend. We don't even know what happens if we wipe out."

"That's stupid. We'd go back to an old save spot or something. Look. Like Amanda said, the pass slopes down as it bends," said Kevin. "You know that's gotta mean we're close to a city. It's gotta be Maniunk."

Amanda huffed and climbed up on the uneven boulders lining the pass. "All right, all right, but after this, no more. If there's no Maniunk, we take a break. I see a trail above that must lead to a Save Point fountain somewhere set in this mountain."

Her companions compromised on this.

Kevin went around the bend first, sliding down in his chainmail boots on some ice, with Donny right behind him. Amanda was to the left and up, ducking down behind white boulders with each change in the pass' layout's nuances.

At the bottom of the bend and slope, twenty Crystal Snow Imps waited. These were bigger and much more fierce than the Snow Imps they had just encountered. Crystal Snow Imps could—and really liked to—go for the throat and kill in one bite, Donny imagined as he looked at their three-inch fangs and claws.

All twenty jumped the heroes at once.

Kevin blocked them and still lost dozens of points in damage; Donny didn't have time to check the exact number because the creatures regrouped and started a second wave, diving for their throats. Donny took 15 in damage, only barely deflecting with a hurried spell. Amanda was knocked to the ground face-down with 11 damage, the only way she wasn't almost instantly killed by the ferocious mini-monsters having been to take the fall.

That's how it started. As a slaughter.

Amanda regained her footing and dodged well, even able to Triple Shot some of the healing Crystal Snow Imps... but there were so many of them. Every time she or Donny got in a hit, another Crystal Snow Imp healed the one they just had zeroed in on. Kevin was soon covered with the things, and all Donny could do was try to Cure Kevin continually and keep him from dying in the attack.

Now Amanda needed help, and Donny had to double his Cures, which left no room for Fireballs or any other offensive spells from looted scrolls. Kevin was Savior the entire time, but still couldn't keep the Crystal Snow Imps off of Amanda and Donny all the way. There simply were too many of them.

And so it went. This was definitely not good.

"How're we supposed to get the hell out of this, Donny?" Amanda yelled to him.

He had no idea. His HP was lower than it had been in a while and was still going down. The timer on his damage counting down from the last Ice Shield hit from a particularly ugly Imp said he had six seconds left of its slow damage-over-time effect. He hastily cast another Cure on himself, and when the time ran out, he had 18HP left.

"We got this! Don't give up!" Kevin yelled, ever the optimist. "Onward, fighters! We will crush you, foes!"

Still, Donny couldn't possibly keep them all alive. There wasn't time. They had to hit the Imps even with the Ice Shields that afflicted their party with the damage-over-time because, otherwise, they'd get hammered by the big moves.

It really looked like Game Over.

Suddenly, the nighttime snowy valley grew somehow darker. It was as though a shadow passed over the hazy glow of the moon through the snow cloud cover.

Donny looked up and saw a figure flying above him. He couldn't make out what it was, but he felt afraid. What new beast was this?

The figure looked like a man each time it flew closer to Donny, and he could make out more, but then in a flash—just as all of their HPs were in the single digits—the shadow figure sped so fast it was a blur.

All their HPs went to full, and all status effects disappeared off Donny's party members.

Next, like from a wave, the Crystal Snow Imps fell over, dead, dead, dead as the figure, Donny now read his name as "Eln" Drained them of vitality.

Donny collapsed in the snow behind Kevin. Amanda had ducked in between two boulders, eyes wide, and peered into the night. Kevin held his battle ax up to the sky, cheering.

"Eln!" Kevin called out. "Great Being of Might, you saved us!"

Donny wasn't as enthusiastic. What was this Eln?

The mysterious shadow figure who flew around and "Drained" the Imps kept himself in the shadows or hidden in the sky, in the low clouds, perhaps. Donny caught glimpses of him out of the corners of his eyes, and then when he looked, Eln was gone.

Amanda crept down from her boulder's advantage and stood next to Donny and Kevin. "I used Insight on him just a sec ago," she said quietly. "He's a Vampire. Level 71. His highest stat is Purpose at 75."

"What does that mean?" Kevin asked. "Where'd he go?"

Nobody said anything as they peered into the dark night sky.

"It's called misdirection," a sleek male voice said behind them. Donny jumped and spun around, wand at the ready, Fireball pulled up in his menu.

The other two did the same.

Eln stood at least seven feet tall and wore a long black velvet cape with a high collar over a blood-red vest, white dress shirt, and black slacks. He had white flesh and deep, penetrating blue eyes like hyacinths wild in an overgrown garden. Two fang tips poked out from his upper lip, lying like sin on his full, red bottom lip. His short, black hair was slicked back, showing a perfect widow's peak on his forehead.

Amanda pulled three arrows back but held off shooting.

Eln waved a long-fingered, white hand at her as though to say *silly you*. "You need not worry yourself with my intentions. I just saved you from horrid deaths. And, as you have seen, I just fed on those dastardly Ice Imps, yet they do not yield much worthwhile blood. Cold, too. However, satisfying enough."

"You fed? But you were in the air, right?" Kevin asked. He wasn't acting scared of Eln in the least. He was rather fascinated, it seemed to Donny.

"My Drain, which I learned at Level 60, allows me to feed from afar. My prey's blood swoops right out of its pathetic body and into me. Do not worry, adventurers from Earth. I am well fed and find you very curious. You are not in my meal plan for now."

"For now," Amanda repeated with a frown, lowering her longbow.

"Most likely not ever, unless you peeve me. You will not peeve me, will you, young Earth female?" he asked Amanda smoothly.

"Uh, no, of course she won't," Donny answered for her in case she got PAF with him. "How do you know we're from Earth?" Changing the subject seemed like the safe thing to do.

"I, too, am from Earth. Serranti, whom I am certain you've heard of, sucked me through his portal while running an experimental test-run."

"Yeah, we hearda him," said Kevin.

"What portal?" Donny asked.

"Were you a vampire on Earth?" Amanda added.

"Yes, I was indeed, a vampire on Earth. Before that, I was human." He looked at Donny. "Like you." He looked around the valley. "Serranti's portal. Dreadful thing. He built it with power from the Life Plant. He connected this world to Earth, and plans to overtake our world with it by sending his Orcs, Trolls, undead, what-have-you, through it. He thinks himself a brilliant battle master and conqueror. He is not, I assure you. I have tasted his filthy blood." Eln ran a slender hand over his slicked-back hair. "After one bite, I would never touch the stuff again. Tainted."

Donny had a million and one questions.

"We didn't come through no portal," Kevin told Eln. "We're playing a game. See?" He held up his ax as though it proved his point.

"A game. Just another sort of portal, if you ask me. How interesting. I would very much like to leave Quintarria and return to Earth. But to do that, I'd have to wait until that tasteless Dark Elf Serranti is able to make the portal work correctly. To make it so he can go through instead of bringing me here. Anyone here. Maybe you?" He cocked an eyebrow at Donny.

"No, Kevin's right. We're playing an Atari game," Donny explained.

"Atari. Intriguing. So, I saved you all, now. What use will you be to me?" Eln folded his long, cloaked arms across his narrow chest.

Amanda said, "We aren't anything to you, so thanks for killing all the Crystal Snow Imps and stuff, but we have to get to Maniunk."

"And what business do you have in the Elven stronghold, young people of Earth playing a game?"

"We're on a quest. Asope, heard of him? He gave us a quest to go to Maniunk," Kevin explained. Donny could tell Kevin had special affection for the strange vampire.

"Probably to get assistance from Lale. Ridiculous. Lale will just give you another quest and make you do his work for him. No matter. You'll never make it within the walls of Maniunk."

"Why? Why do you say that?" Donny asked.

Eln shook his head. "The Ruby Dragon guards the only gate into the Elven stronghold. That's why Serranti and his ghouls haven't taken that last Elven city. The Ruby Dragon is a good dragon, brought to being from the Life Plant long ago when the Elves tended it. The Ruby Dragon will not let you pass, and you are simply too weak to fight it."

"You've mentioned this Life Plant twice now," Donny said. "I'm curious about what it is."

"Maybe, if you happen to defeat the Ruby Dragon by some lucky chance, Lale can explain the Life Plant. I know not of its details, just that the Elves once held it, and three thousand years ago, Serranti took hold of it. It has magical properties the Elves, both light and dark, utilize. From what I understand, nobody in Quintarria can comprehend what the Life Plant actually is nor what it is capable of." Eln unfolded his arms, eying Donny. "I enjoy seeing another human. It has been many moons since I've seen a human face. Tell me your names."

They did.

Donny added, "How much do you like seeing a human face?" An idea had occurred to him. Amanda gave him a weird look as he asked, as though she were afraid the question would urge the vampire Eln into launching his bite to Donny's neck for some sweet, sweet human blood.

"Donny, I very much enjoy it. You are young. I was once young and am reminded of this. I was happy when I was young and alive." He traced a finger down his cheek and smiled slightly at the clouds above.

"Well, you helped us. You saved our lives. And you're from our world, so we owe you one. We're on the same team, right?" Donny urged, nodding up at the vampire.

"That's right, Eln. We're totally on the same team," Kevin added with a grin, not at all aware of Donny's ploy. It worked in Donny's favor. This was a game, and Eln was a character who already said he was motivated by favors, yet was for Team Earth.

In fact, he wanted to get back there.

"You children are too weak to be of much help to me, I'm afraid," Eln dodged, frowning at Donny.

He gave it a try anyway. "We can figure out a way to get you back to Earth if you can get us past the Ruby Dragon," he said, eying Eln carefully, holding his cards close.

"How do you intend to do that?" Eln asked, and then leaned to the side. "I'm listening."

"You're not like us. Did you know we go back and forth? Between here and Earth? I can do it right now if I want. Did you know that?" Donny said in a rush, not wanting to lose Eln's attention for a second.

"Oh?" He stood straight. "Is this so?" he asked Kevin. "You and you?" He looked at Amanda.

"All three of us, that's right," Kevin said.

"How is this magic accomplished?"

"It's a game. I told you," Kevin said.

"Wait, hang on, Kevin. I don't think he knows what a game is." Donny held up a hand to Kevin, shushing him. He turned to Eln. "A game is a type of Earth magic discovered in our time. We can go, uh, in and out of worlds. With technology… and magic."

Eln's eyes penetrated Donny. Kevin stared at Donny with confusion, and Amanda had tightened the grip on her bow.

"You are a Wizard. You are also the leader. You are a human Wizard who possesses this magic."

"That's right, Eln. I do."

Amanda relaxed. "I should get some credit. I made the damn thing work."

"You know the technology Don speaks of?" Eln said to her.

"Yeah. I do. You could say that." She smiled proudly, then winked at Donny. "Are you going to help us kick a dragon's ass, and let Donny here work on figuring out a way to use his human Wizard magic to get you back to Earth?"

Eln smirked at her. "You know I must, persistent girl. No wonder you have a way with technology. It has the basis of one man's way of thinking at its core, and its applications are left for the rest who learn of his ideas, fabricate and actualize the implementations for design with the earth's materials, objects, that are guesses at how to utilize best in the way that one person thought brilliantly at one time, singularly. All cultures with technology are built on its first thinker whose thoughts were heard. Word of mouth is everything, and last I was on Earth, the radio was a new technology never seen in many eons. It had been designed somewhat similarly in ages or places I experienced it in my 80,000 years as a vampire on Earth. I have gathered how much time has passed by your speech and terminology, and am assured you are from around one hundred years at most in my future. With the kind of mass communication like radio, ideas spread faster than they are dreamt of, and many brilliant minds find many applications easily with help or without. But still, I see no new basis for what drives your technology as of your time. You are persistent like one who manipulates alternating electrical current as a power source."

He sighed. "However, it is a wonderful sign to know civilization survived its most recent foray into such communications. Most of the time, everything gets torn to pieces within twenty years."

Donny and the other two listened, stunned, and Donny was admittedly fascinated with this character's speech. It was like he really knew stuff. Neat.

"You got it, Eln," said Donny.

"Couldn'ta said it better myself," Kevin added. "You do words good."

"Thank you, Kevin. You do words good, as well. Or, as good. I'm hesitant to know if you understand me, for I have trouble following your dialect and word choices." He shook his head. "No matter. It is disconcerting, but I believe you, Donny, are my only hope for returning to Earth. Not Serranti's portal."

"Why couldn't you have forced him to put you back? You're a high-level vampire who can suck the blood out of a body from a distance. That's crazy," said Kevin.

Eln tilted his head at Kevin. "I could never defeat him and rule him. As I said, I tried his blood. It's not as though the idea didn't occur to me. He has too many allies. His life is to have allies to crush enemies with."

"So, he has to have both," Amanda said. "Allies, and enemies to crush."

"Why, certainly, Amanda. That is exactly correct. I have no such need, nor allies. I have many enemies, for Elves and Dark Elves live long lives, and there's one I've met who has memory from the beginning of time to the end of it. He's a rare one in an ice age.

"I will assist you further by helping you with the Ruby Dragon, and then I will take my leave. Lale will not like me in his stronghold. Do not ask; it doesn't matter. Nobody ever forgets a vampire's misdeeds, but their own are to be understood, acknowledged and validated for them. I will come to you another time, when there are no such judgments. Come. Now. Maniunk is only thirty feet west. The Elves fill the pass here heavily with Snow Imps as protection and to feed the Ruby Dragon. The Elves call it keeping a life cycle." He chuckled then spun away, walking boldly toward the narrow, dark passage that had been just beyond the twenty Snow Imps moments ago.

There was a dragon in its darkness, and because of the now-heavy snowfall, Donny couldn't see anything but Eln disappearing into a black hole in white just as a flashing sparkle star of deep red shone around him for an instant in silhouette. Yeah, there was a dragon, and its scales must be made of rubies, and it was moving... close. That's why the flash was so fast. And then there. Another. Kevin's red chainmail brightened in reflection near Eln.

Amanda was nowhere to be seen.

He picked up the pace and followed, wand at the ready, practicing the moves to choices in his menu, memorizing exact wording, to be prepared for anything.

CHAPTER 4

Donny thought it was ridiculous that some people thought dragons existed, had ever existed, or could possibly exist on other planets or in other dimensions of time and space. Therefore, it never even occurred to him he could possibly see a dragon ever, ever in his whole entire life.

Donny saw a dragon, the Ruby Dragon, and it was now a she. She saw them, too, but kept her blue-black sapphire eyes locked on Donny's own. She took no notice of Eln nor Kevin, and Amanda was doing her stealth thing. Donny had a feeling the Ruby Dragon still knew where Amanda was, but all she cared about was sizing Donny up.

"It's because you're a human," Eln said between the dragon's loud, angry snorts that shook the walls of the mountainside cave tunnel leading to Maniunk. "She knows not your image nor smell, and as I said, she is a good dragon. Does this word 'good' have a completely different meaning so soon?" He shook his head. "Ruby Dragon," he called out. She didn't look at him. She stayed crouched on four long, angular ruby-scaled, monstrous legs, huge red wings with white underneath hesitating to take action, one lengthy, narrow, brilliantly red ear turned at Eln. She snuffed hard, waiting…

Watching Donny. He felt her deep blue eyes assessing his core being. It actually felt like he was meeting a dragon. Like an alien from another planet. Another species, and they were checking each other out. Except the Ruby Dragon was getting a much bigger picture of him than Donny was of her. It was in the slight wavering, dilating of the blackest of black slit pupils, continuous and fast as she looked at him as though appraising art.

Donny was seeing a dragon, and right then, dragons were real.

"I wish Amanda were here," muttered Kevin, ax and shield ready. "She could Insight her and tell us." Donny wasn't surprised that Kevin knew the Ruby Dragon was a she, too.

"Not many dragons assist. The Ruby Dragon can't be higher than level 30," Eln said casually while examining his perfect fingernails.

The Ruby Dragon shot gray smoke out of her nostrils, continuing to eye Donny.

He felt like he needed to do something. "Uh, hello, Ruby Dragon. I'm Donny. I'm here to see Lale, the Elf. Asope, a half-Elf, told me to find him in the city you guard. I don't suppose… you'd let us pass?" He smiled weakly, not able to pull off not being afraid.

"She ain't gonna. Look at her. She's sizing you up, Don. Watch out," said Kevin. "Want me to Savior before she goes for you?"

Donny shook his head. "Wait. Let's see what she does first."

"I wouldn't advise that," Eln told Donny just as the Ruby Dragon swept up from the icy ground and flew into the air of the cavern above them. The wind from her wings blew Donny's robes like he was in a tornado. Even Kevin said, "Whoa," at the force of the wind.

"Now you've done it," Eln commented, still not taking action and seeming unconcerned.

The Ruby Dragon rolled her red-horned head around and then opened her sharp-toothed mouth, aiming for Donny and Kevin. A blast of bright red flame spewed from her maw.

Ruby Dragon uses Red Fire on Donny and Kevin. Donny and Kevin take 72 damage.

"Wow!" Kevin yelled.

Kevin used Savior right away, much to Donny's relief, but the Ruby Dragon shot streaks of red light out of her eyes and stunned Kevin for 10 seconds, so the game chat log said.

"Oh, my, my," said Eln. "Whatever are you to do now?"

"Let me show you—it's called a *Fireball*!" Donny wound up like a major league pitcher and cast a monster of a Fireball spell, the biggest he had ever thrown or any of his band of adventurers had ever even *seen*.

It did absolutely nothing. Could dragons laugh? It definitely sounded like the Ruby Dragon was laughing.

Donny's mouth hung agape. "What in the seven realms?"

"She's a *dragon*. Do you really think *fire* is going to hurt her?" Eln said with an exaggerated yawn.

It was a good point. As if to punctuate it, the Ruby Dragon swiped down with her left paw and scratched her enormous red claws across Donny's chest, making streaks of blood bloom and taking him down over 50 damage points.

Donny quickly Cured Kevin, and then himself. At least the monster couldn't do damage from a dist—

Whomp! The dragon slammed Donny with the Crystal Stare and stunned him in place for what felt like an eternity, but was in fact only ten long seconds.

"Got anything else, Wizard?" Eln asked, bored. "Or any of you, for that matter?"

Amanda rushed up and tried her trusty Triple Shot, but the creature barely noticed, suffering just 30 HP damage.

"*Eln!*" Amanda yelled at him. "What the hell are you doing? I thought you were going to help us!"

The Ruby Dragon flapped her massive wings, opened her maw, and shot out fire studded with what must have been rocks—no, *rubies*. It made sense, Donny thought, even as the huge, uncut red stones smashed into them, taking them each down at least 40 HP and stunning them for ten years.

Kevin shook himself out of it first and tossed his ax in a Slice move. The dragon was far enough away that the ax sailed by, returning to the Dwarf like a boomerang.

Next, Donny awoke and Cured Kevin immediately.

"Eln, you should be ashamed of yourself!" Amanda chided angrily as she pulled back three arrows.

Amanda uses Triple Shot on Ruby Dragon. Ruby Dragon takes 33 damage.

"She has 370 HP, guys!" Amanda called out, pulling back more arrows.

"She's about to burn you again," Eln explained. "Surely one of you will die."

Donny turned to Eln after curing Amanda. "Eln, please. Don't you want me to help you?"

The Ruby Dragon spewed Red Fire at Amanda, doing a good bit of damage.

"You dastardly creature!" Kevin yelled, ax held high.

"Very well. I wanted to see what you are capable of. Not much, apparently." Eln flew into the air at the flying red dragon in a streak of black.

Eln Bites Ruby Dragon. Ruby Dragon takes 66 damage.

Eln Drains Ruby Dragon. Ruby Dragon takes 103 damage.

The beast didn't seem to know what to do with herself. She couldn't target the speeding Eln.

"See? No more than Level 30, as I said." Eln flew right at the massive beast again in a shot.

Eln uses Eternal Kiss on Ruby Dragon. Ruby Dragon dies.

The great, impossible monster dragon fell from the air and landed on the icy cave floor with an earth-shaking thud. She stayed unmoving.

"Lale hated me before. Now he'll have an army after me," Eln complained, landing gracefully next to the Ruby Dragon's body just as it faded, like all things did when they were killed in Quest. "I must bid you farewell. In moments, Elves will be everywhere, and I've fed too much. She had delectable blood, I must say. Generally, I do not feed on dragons. I dislike fire, as you can imagine." He turned to Donny. "I trust you will keep your promise, and I will find you again somewhere in your travels to see what progress you have made in our pact."

Eln flew back into the air and zoomed out of the back of the cave passage, and then disappeared like he'd never been there.

The other side of the dark path inside the mountainside wall was lit with torchlights. Lots of them. Too many of them, coming their way. Elves by the dozens crowded into the cavern. The three Earthlings had some questions to answer.

*

Donny thought Lale must be very old, because unlike other Elves, who looked like his sister, his eyes glowed bright yellow and had no pupils. His hair was a flowing mane of orangish-yellow tamed flames. His pale flesh glowed softly like candlelight, which made his pointy Elven features stand out in stark contrast. He wore a crimson robe with the hood down, trimmed in silver and gold.

The Elf, Lale, sat across a square white-wood table from them on a patio of the Tower of Maniunk. The best patio, Donny thought, because he could see every bit of the city from the high vantage point as the sun rose over the eastern mountains of its border. Carved ice covered the buildings. Donny had no idea what kind of maintenance the meticulous and beautiful carvings required. Everything glistened with the new day's light, and the steepled structures under him gave illumination from below as it came from above. Mountains rose on all sides of the city of Maniunk, ensuring protection from everywhere but the entrance Donny had come through... and was involved in killing the safeguard for.

Everything had a bluish hue to it from the layers of ice, and Lale quietly explained how the Elves used ice as insulation with magic. There had been nothing but silence for five minutes before Lale spoke.

Interesting way to open that up, Donny thought, but it was a game, and in this game, that wasn't so unusual. They'd all been waiting since the Elves with the torches in the Ruby Dragon's cavern demanded an explanation, and Donny would only say, "Asope sent us to see Lale," until one of them heard, and all fell silent.

They'd been taken through the ice city to the palace and told to sit at the square table where Lale already waited.

"How is ice insulation? That's crazy," Kevin said.

"Shut up, Kevin," Amanda hissed.

Lale opened the burning book in front of him. "You can tell them, Amanda. Tell them what your Insight tells you of me." He seemed to begin reading from the book to himself.

"Level 60. Intellect at 67. He's a Fire Mage. I guess that's why he's all like... that. And he does damage. Big damage. All fire damage." She raised an eyebrow at Donny.

"I'm sorry we killed your dragon," Donny said, feeling guilty even though he hadn't done the deed. He knew he would have, though, for the quest, if he'd been strong enough. Seeing this city and these Elves, and now Lale, he realized these were a people who were afraid and lived isolated for protection. They had no freedom.

"How is it three Level 21s killed the Ruby Dragon?" He looked up from his book to Donny. His voice had a gentle echo to it.

"Just luck, I guess." Donny thought fast. He didn't want Eln to get in any trouble. Donny asked him to help. It was his idea. "We woke her," he lied. "Maybe that was it. She was surprised."

Kevin and Amanda looked at him, but said nothing. They seemed to want to protect Eln, too.

"Asope would not send you to me unless it was important. Did he tell you what he sent you for?"

"No, it was our next quest, your majesty," Kevin answered.

"Ah," Lale said with a nod. Flames fell around his cheeks. "Asope never sends anyone on a quest. But we've all been waiting for him to take action. This must be an advantage he sees that ensured him success.

"I am not of help to you now except to give you another quest. One I cannot take part in, not yet. The Ruby Dragon is dead. I must guard Maniunk's entrance until we can find another guardian. I am the only one with such magic left in this city. You must know this. There was a war. The Elven War. The half-Elves, led by Serranti... have you heard of him?"

"A little," Donny said.

"Serranti, through Warlock magic, tricked the minds of the three Elves tending to the Life Plant. I was one of them. He asserted control over it, did not and still does not tend to it. He uses it, and it will eventually die, but he cares not. I am steering off topic.

"In the Elven War, Serranti already had the Life Plant, and with it, gave sentience to the Trolls and undead living in the deep places of Quintarria. He communicated with the Orcs. The Dwarves knew of them, but saw them as pests, contained them. Once they had sentience, and also were trained by Warlock magic to be loyal eternally to Serranti, they formed societies bent on serving Serranti. The Elves stood no chance against the Dark Elves and the creatures from the deep Serranti changed to fight with him. It was a slaughter.

"Those of us who survived retreated here to Maniunk, the stronghold of the four Elven cities. Elves never trusted the Dark Elves, for their spirits are linked to the dead and the endings of things. Elves' spirits are linked to the living and its cycles. That is how I can explain it to you.

"Do not fret over the Ruby Dragon. We knew it was a fault that, were help to come, the Ruby Dragon is not tame. She is her own being. She was. The risk was always there that something like this would happen."

He got to the point, Donny thought, but Donny couldn't stop sitting on the edge of his gold-gilded white-wood seat.

"Now, for your next quest, one Asope would want me to explain to you, you must take back the Dark Elf cities of Sillia to the south, Laranda to the east, and unite Pariss to the north. There will be help with Pariss. The Alliance was slavery; it has now ended certain terms, and the freed half-Elf slaves are not institutionalized. They have been alive for thousands of years. Blood more Dark Elf, perhaps, but they are of thoughts of life.

"Start with Sillia to the south. Rumor is that the Dark Elf leader of Sillia might have turned against Serranti. This is a weakness you must exploit.

"We have the Diamond Dragon here, as well, and he is tame, educated. He will take you beyond the mountain range and into warmer climes. From there," his glowing eyes turned to Amanda, "use your Elven eyes for unnoticed trails to Sillia. You must find a way inside, and you have yet to gain true powers in your leveling." He looked at the three of them for a moment. "You need fighting experience, but you also need not get caught by patrols on common roads." He turned back to Donny.

"Human, you have great gifts. Only you and your party can do this, otherwise Asope never would have sent you to me. Now, no time to waste. We go to the forested area you see below, over there." He pointed.

"The Diamond Dragon lives in that wood. We go to him, and then you take flight."

"Take flight?" Kevin asked. "You mean, we're gonna fly on the dragon?"

Lale tilted his fiery head at Kevin. "Yes. Indeed, yes. You will find it not in the least dangerous, Dwarf."

"Are you kidding me?" Kevin said. "I can't wait!"

"First," Amanda said, "we need a Save Point fountain. Got one around here? I gotta pee, guys."

CHAPTER 5

Kevin had given archaic battle cries all through the ride on the Diamond Dragon, a beast that looked like it was made of huge carved and polished diamonds. Its skin was just as hard, too, and twinkled like a miner's dream.

The dragon took them southeast of Maniunk, and somehow that frigid place was close to a dry, desert area beyond the foothills and, being lower and out of the mountains, it made sense to Donny that it could be a desert. Twisty, gnarled trees four feet high here and there, with scraggly brush all around was the barren land before them.

In this place, even before the Diamond Dragon disappeared from view in the sky as it flew back to Maniunk, they were attacked by Nomad Cactuses. They had a move called Needles where they threw bundles of cactus needles at Donny's party. Kevin's Block came in especially handy. Donny Cured mostly, with a few Fireballs, and Amanda used Triple Shot from hiding spots between tan, dusty boulders or desperate, scraggly trees.

"When will I get to use these knives?" she complained at one point, trying yet again to get one out of the death grip of her leather belt.

On they continued, fighting cactuses, and then as the landscape changed to rainfall and jungle over the course of an hour's travel, they fought the undead. Donny found them creepy at first. There were thieves, archers, mages, and rogues. They looked like they'd been some mix of body-builder human and deformed Dark Elf, and they were rotted to different degrees. None of them had eyes—just empty eye-sockets.

It seemed they'd traveled and battled for hours and hours, but at the same time, it was so fun that time flew. Donny kept waiting for Amanda to call it a day and quit playing, insist on finding a Save Point fountain, but so far, she hadn't. He wasn't going to remind her of her so, so important plans that night, whatever they might be.

He admitted to himself he couldn't play this game without her. Not without Kevin, either, the dork.

With the desert behind them and jungle growth thick around them, Amanda found hidden trails with her Elven eyes, now with mostly undead monsters to fight on their way southeast to Sillia. At one point, they were ambushed by a group of six undead that seemed to be in a band. They wore better-looking armor than the other undead they'd fought. They definitely were close to Sillia. That had to be a patrol.

Donny, Kevin, and Amanda were Level 29 at that point, and, with each level, their hits got stronger, and Donny's Cures healed more HP. These undead seemed weak now, compared to how they'd been when Donny's party entered the jungle close to Sillia. They took out the six undead in a one-minute battle, and within a few seconds of the last one dying, they were all full HP. They had a rhythm to this.

It was dusk when they arrived near Sillia. Couldn't miss it. It clung to, no, it *was* the top and sides of a cliff overlooking a beautiful, bright blue sea. A calm water. Sillia had been carved from the granite of the cliff in fanciful patterns, like it had been designed by a geologist who used his master's degree to make architecture. One Elf must have made this city, maybe even in moments, with some magic, long ago, because it had a consistent yet arcane style. The windows to the houses were all spirals spinning different ways outward from a center point, usually a circular doorway, open, or an ornate rock ladder for the occupants to climb to their large, dipping roofs and have a… cold one? *What would they do up there?* Donny wondered.

"How the hell are we going to get in there? Every spiral window has an undead face in it. Look," Amanda complained. "We don't even have any new abilities. I mean, we just got to Level 30. The last abilities we got were sixteen levels ago. Jesus." She folded her muscular, leather-bound arms across her bountiful chest. Donny noticed she stuck it out more in the game. As if, he thought, because out of this game, Amanda didn't have it. He snickered.

"What, goon?" she said suspiciously. "You're being an asshole somehow. I know that laugh. Come on, okay. Fine. There's a small trail right here that looks like all the other ones I've seen that lead to Save Point fountains. It has to be time for Mom to get home."

"It's not," said Kevin.

"What the hell do you know, freak?" she said, bored.

"I peeked over my goggles at the cuckoo clock. Said 5:15. See? You know how this works. We can get in there, take over, get out, and then you can save. What you got going on that's better than this? I mean, what could possibly be better than this?" Kevin cocked his intimidating Dwarf head up at her.

"Just stuff, okay?"

"Amanda always has stuff," Donny added.

"Shut up. You never shut up enough."

"Come on, Amanda. Just a little bit longer. Please," Kevin begged. "We must conquer and save the lands of Quintarria!" His voice boomed.

She looked up at the cliff city of Sillia in the distance. "Okay, only if we figure out a way to do it right, and how to do it right, fast. I don't want to sit here and talk about it for two hours of Quintarria time, whatever the hell is up with that." She sat on a moss-covered log and played with a frond from a giant fern hanging next to her.

Kevin squatted with one knee up, and the other knee balanced in the air an inch from the foliage by his left foot suspended just so on its tippy-toes. Since when did Kevin do that? He looked like a jock.

"So?" Amanda asked Donny. "You're the Wizard. You're supposed to be the smart one. What next? Knock on the rock gate? 'Hey! There are three killers out here. Let us in!'"

Donny shrugged and sat cross-legged amidst intersecting ground-creeper vines, with big, green leaves and fat, pink flowers. He had to come up with something before his sister got bored again and thought more about her important stuff. Or Mom coming home. Or anything. She'd ruin it. Donny wasn't an idiot. He could do this. He could figure it out.

But he didn't have to.

A voice from a nearby thick tree trunk behind Amanda and out of Donny's view said, "You can't walk into Sillia. Not an Elf. A Dwarf? Maybe. A human? I highly doubt you'd make it five steps once a Dark Elf lays eyes on you.

"The Elf would die, the Dwarf would have to choose to fight or play the part of trader, and you, Donny, human, would be taken. Taken as a gift." The voice had a soft timbre, high for a male voice, but not too high. Donny figured it was more how it lilted through high and low notes like a song that made the stranger sound this way.

They all looked at the tree's base, where huge ferns had parted, and there stood a half-Elf. He was tall, with long, long solid white hair falling over his shoulders and onto his chest, pale blue skin, and pointed ears that stood out from his head, parting his hair in a way that made him look devious. He wore a black leather suit similar to Amanda's, but it had buckles up the front instead of the sides, silver and shined to a mirror-finish. In one hand, he held a great, knotty, thick staff with a white, glowing stone in its clawed top, and in the other, pointing down, he held a three-foot blade that flashed in waves like it had smooth, white flames coming off it, probably from an enchantment. He had a dagger slid in the front of his belt, no sheath. Easy to get to.

"My name is Melarrine, and you can trust I have no love for Dark Elves. You must have learned by now that half-Elves rarely do." He smiled and nodded, waiting for them to say something.

"He's Level 56," said Amanda. "Half-Elf Wizard-Knight, whatever that is. Highest is Purpose at 54, but Strength and Defense are at 52."

"I don't mind your using Insight on me," said Melarrine, taking a small step forward. Kevin hopped up from his crouch. Donny wondered why. Melarrine seemed fine. Asope was half-Elf, and Lale said half-Elves thought of themselves as victims and slaves, right? Because of the Dark Elves? The alliance?

Melarrine continued, still smiling. "Amanda, you are a beautiful young Elf. What exquisite hair you have."

She lowered her eyebrows for a second, then rolled her eyes. "Your hair's pretty rad, too."

"Thank you. And you, Kevin. You are the bravest Dwarf I've met, and I'm nearly three thousand years old. No Dwarf has ever come this close to Sillia since the Dark Elves took it, except for the greediest ones who sneaked out of the underground cities with gold figures formed from the Red Dragon's breath. Not bravery, greed. They knew that in Sillia, these were treasures, and many fine gems that can only be mined in the cliffs of Sillia will trade hands for them. These Dwarves hide their treasure when they find it mining, form the dragon-breath gold, waiting for a day to turn it into better, newer treasure. Yes, Dwarf? Not you, though. You have honor." He had made his way to them until he stood next to Amanda.

"So, what? What's so great about my little brother? Isn't it his turn for you to tell him what's great about him? Who are you and what do you want?" Amanda asked, jaw set. Still, she didn't touch her bow. It stayed at her hip, and her thin fingers off her arrows.

Melarrine laughed. "Some might think you, Amanda, have the Dark Elf blood around here. You must know I mean no harm. I have been sent to assist you. No need to know who sent me. An admirer who wishes to reveal himself at a later time. Yes. He must keep his whereabouts secret at all times. He is a wanted Elf. I can say no more about him except I serve you at his request."

"Serve us? How?" Kevin asked, leaning on his ax, meaty hands dangling over the sharp, thick blade.

"To help you with your quest."

"How do you know about our quest?" Donny asked.

"Half-Elves know about you in some circles. The kinds of circles who always hear of something like a human coming to Quintarria. I beg of you, do not speak my name to another Elf or half-Elf. I am to keep my whereabouts unknown as well, for reasons I will explain at another time. First, I will offer my assistance to your current quest." He sheathed his sword as it lost its glowing enchantment.

Donny didn't like how Melarrine kept changing the subject when anyone asked him a question—or was he just saying a whole lot and, in the course of that, the subject changed? Donny couldn't be sure, come to think about it.

Maybe Melarrine was a character like Eln, and was designed by the game for them to do this part of the quest with. Could be. Donny would have to mention it to Amanda and Kevin when they weren't playing. There had to be patterns in Quest. All games had patterns. Every single one.

"We can't do crap in Sillia without any new abilities. Melarrine, how do we get new abilities? Asope gave us our last ones, and the others we had when we got our races and classes," Amanda said, sounding irritated with him for no reason. Maybe, Donny thought, it was her usual couldn't-care-less attitude she put on when she was being the cool punk rock bass player with her little idolizers.

"What level are you, young Elf?" Melarrine asked her.

"We're all Level 30. We, like, literally just turned Level 30 last fight."

Melarrine's stance changed slightly. Or did Donny imagine it?

"Just now, before we began speaking?"

Amanda shrugged. "Yeah, something like that. It wasn't long ago, and we killed three undead rogues. Easy as pie." She plucked the string on her bow and tossed her bluish-white hair. *Yeah, totally being the rock star,* Donny thought.

Melarrine took a step back. "You gain new abilities every ten levels starting at Level 30, but nobody will come to give them to you when I'm here." He took two more steps back, and ferns began covering his arms and legs.

"What do you mean?" Kevin asked. "Hey, wait, don't go. Who's coming?"

"You know who. At least, I think you do. I may be wrong. We all learn from someone different. I'll go now, find you soon." He spun and faded into the heavy jungle growth, calling behind him, "Trust me, it's the way things work."

It was just the three of them again.

"Well, Donny, now what?" Amanda said.

"Hey, Donny's just the party leader. He doesn't know the game or nothin'. None of us have ever played it," Kevin said.

Donny thought it was funny that Kevin stood up for him to his sister. "Don't worry, Kevin. Amanda just likes making her bad moods my fault if I'm around. I don't know who the lucky person is when I'm not."

"You're the shit who read my diary last year. Mom never would have known I took the overnight road trip for a show in Nashville if you hadn't told her."

"It was an accident. I was only thirteen. I thought she knew."

"No, you didn't, goon. You told."

"Stop, now, young ones." A familiar, warm voice stopped the conversation dead.

"Asope!" Donny said, being the first to spy him coming from the secret trail Amanda had led them to this spot from.

"Asope, finally," Amanda said. "It's good to see you."

"She really thinks so," said Kevin. "She doesn't sound pissed as a pistol anymore."

"Shut up, Kevin," Amanda told the kid. She turned back to Asope as he entered their established little glade.

He put his bluish, long hand on Donny's shoulder.

"I've been on your trail ever since I was in Pariss. I kept track through spies. I teleported just now when it was safe. I went undetected. There are eyes on me always. I cannot stay, but I had to find you. I'm sorry I'm late." He looked deep into Donny's eyes, worried.

"Late for what?" Donny asked.

"Late being here to give you your new abilities. Your Level 30 abilities. I initiated your quest. I assigned your first new abilities, ones that don't come from your choices with Howlinowa."

"What is that guy?" Kevin said. "I don't mind it's not him giving us abilities and it's you. I like you. That Game Host guy is creepy. Who talks to three people and doesn't show his face?"

Asope smiled at Kevin. "Howlinowa can be unnerving, especially with those miniature human skulls on the ropes hanging around his neck. Odd one, Howlinowa. He's Level 0, all stats are at 0, but he's never been seen except by a select few. He comes in secret places, and rarely, only when absolutely necessary."

"Necessary for what? The quest?" Kevin asked.

"Necessary for the game Quest is more like it," Amanda muttered.

"I've only seen him once, and that was when I hunted him down to find a way to help the Elves. There's another time and place for that. I remember Level 30. I know you want your abilities." He grinned and held out his free, thin, blue-tinted white hand, tossed his light brown hair out of an eye, rows of gold hoop earrings flashing with the movement.

"Yeah," Kevin said, putting his shield and ax down, and rubbing his hands together. "Hit me with it."

Asope chuckled. "Okay, Kevin, you first. I grant you the ability Shield Bash. You do damage with this blocking offensive move."

Kevin plucked his shield off the ground so fast Donny thought it might have been made of chocolate and the fat Dwarf couldn't wait. Speaking of...

"Kevin, what did you do with that food Asope gave you last time?"

Kevin dropped his shield, which he'd been turning and examining as though it had the ability. Stupid kid didn't even open his scroll first. "Oh, I totally forgot about it."

"That's okay," Asope said. "Best to save, and a Dwarf knows how to save. I have another food item to assist your Appetite race-specific if you ever use it. The time will come when you will remember. This time, I offer you Pigmy Pie. It is made of the magic dust fey pigmies spread. Baked into a spiced pumpkin pie. It boosts your Strength stat by 12 for ten minutes."

"Man, no way. I won't forget that one. Thanks, Asope," said Kevin, looking at the entire pie in his hands before putting it in his bag.

"Amanda," Asope continued, "we don't have much time. I cannot stay in one place too long. To you I grant the ability Throw Knives."

"I can finally use these freaking things? Excellent," she said, easily pulling one out of her belt. Before, she hadn't been able to. "Throw them, huh?"

"As I said, range is your strength. Look at your scroll. You will find, through experience, when knife or when bow is the most effective weapon in different ways with all kinds of foes."

Amanda opened her stat scroll and read. Aloud, she muttered, "Agility, Strength with Throw Knives. I wonder…" She trailed off without finishing.

Asope hadn't taken his hand from Donny's shoulder, and now he looked down into Donny's eyes. "I give to you, Donny, a spell you will need now—Resurrect. This spell will bring anyone back from the dead as long as you catch them before they fade. Your Earth companions, Amanda and Kevin, will not fade, however. They are who you need it for most. My advice? Always keep yourself Cured before your party members." He patted Donny's shoulder and let go.

"I must be on my way. It's time. Congratulations on making it to Level 30 on your quest. May you continue to find success, and may your foes fall swiftly." He nodded at each of them, waved a hand.

Asope casts Teleport. Asope vanishes.

Whoosh!

"That's interesting," Amanda said. "Hey, Donny, you're kind of a mage. Wonder if you'll get to teleport."

Donny doubted it. He hadn't figured out the difference between Mages, Wizards, and Warlocks yet, as all had been introduced or mentioned, like Serranti of the Warlock ways. And Lale was a Fire Mage, a specific kind of Mage, while this new Melarrine was a Wizard-Knight, and God knew what he did with all those flashy weapons. He bet Amanda knew. She always said what Insight told her as far as level, high stats, and class. What did she see when she looked at their abilities? What about the stats listed next to them? What did those mean?

Donny opened his scroll.

Donny—Human—Wizard—Level 30

Strength: 34

Defense: 26

Agility: 26

Intellect: 42

Charm: 29

Purpose: 41

Hit Points (Maximum Health): ***310/310HP***

Power of One (Race Specific)—Purpose

Storm Rage (Class Specific)—Strength, Intellect

Fireball—Strength, Intellect

Cure—Purpose, Intellect

Resurrect—Purpose, Intellect

Did those two stats listed with the spells and abilities mean something? Donny had a feeling it had to do with how his stats leveled, or didn't level up, when he did. He noticed that the higher his Purpose went, the more HP his Cures healed. Or was it the other way around? His Cures made his Purpose higher? He'd ask Amanda. She would be a smartass about it, but she'd be able to figure it out, especially with all the times she used Insight. She must have made some connections.

"Huh," Kevin said, also looking at his stat scroll. "My Defense is higher than my Strength by but three points. My Defense is at 40, and my Strength is at 38."

"Idiot. That's two points," Amanda pointed out.

"Still. My Defense keeps going up no matter what. And my Strength, too. Just what I'd want to be better."

"You are a clever group." It was Melarrine's voice, coming from right behind Donny. He spun around and looked up into the half-Elf's black eyes.

"Oh, oh. Hey, Melarrine. Didn't expect you to… how did you know to come back? Were you watching?"

"Of course, he was watching. I call it spying. Anyway, Melarrine," said Amanda, flipping one of her throwing knives in the air and catching it by the blade with one hand. "How do you intend on helping us with these services you say you have to offer?"

Melarrine patted Donny on the shoulder like Asope did, but whereas Asope was warm and reassuring, Melarrine seemed desperate to be accepted, making actions, saying things so that they would react positively to him. The best way Donny could put it was that Melarrine wanted them to think he was one of them. From what Donny understood of half-Elves, if Melarrine was as old as he said, then he'd broken the rules of the Vople Nole'on Alliance a long, long time ago, and who knew who he served now? Who else had their fingers in this quest Donny and his party worked so hard to complete? Who had stakes?

"Thinking like a Wizard, Donny," said Melarrine. "I know how a Wizard thinks. A Wizard-Knight is both a Wizard and a Knight, but there are different spells, abilities, class-specifics. You'll see it yourself, because I'm going to sneak the three of you into Sillia. I know a way in. Money talks to Dark Elves, but not so much to the undead. That's why I spent the last few months coming here and feeling out the Dark Elves who travel out of Sillia, come to the jungle for whatever business they don't want done in Sillia under Neea's watch. I've scouted a way into the city."

"Neea? Who's she?" Donny asked.

"Neea is Serranti's first great-grandchild. Dark Elf. She holds the city in the name of Serranti, but I have uncovered she's betrayed him. She makes plans even now to take the Life Plant from him. But enough of that. No time.

"I made an acquaintance with a Dark Elf citizen of Sillia who has a cliff-dwelling of his very own, accessible by rope, if he places it there. While I was gone and you gained abilities, I arranged with him through Surrey Bird Messaging that he place the rope, so we must go, and now, before his rope is spotted and questioned. Yes. But it is late, and harder to see, so we have that advantage. Now, come, come with me. Into Sillia, and I'll lead you to where Neea stays. If you defeat Neea, who has turned all the undead in her favor, and against Serranti without his yet knowing, the undead will then follow you. I help you this way. I will help you defeat Neea. Now, let's go." He gestured and walked toward the edge of jungle between the high drop-off to the calm sea and the flora's edge, with the obvious intent of getting under those strange and exotically carved home fronts on the edge of the city of Sillia.

CHAPTER 6

"God, my thumb hurts," Amanda said under her breath.

"Don't you play Atari ever?" Kevin asked. "You gotta build up your thumb."

"I know that, idiot. I play as much as I want. This is excessive."

"Not for me. My thumb doesn't hurt at all. How about you, Don?"

"My thumb's fine."

"Stop talking about thumbs and move up the rope, dweebs."

"You started talking about thumbs," Kevin pointed out.

"Just move." Amanda was last on the rope as they climbed up to the Dark Elf's home in Sillia. Melarrine was in the lead. Donny had a hard time wiggling the joystick right at first, and it peeved Amanda that he was slow. Then he had it, and there was no problem. Up he shimmied.

Once inside the Dark Elf's home, Donny saw that, although the lights were on, there was no Dark Elf. Maybe he hid just in case they got caught and he could say he didn't know anything about it.

The room's furnishings were completely made of carved rock. Not even a pillow in that place. The round door to the alley to their right stood open, and Donny saw nobody, heard nobody.

"What do we do, Melarrine?"

He pulled out his sword.

Melarrine casts Ice Blade. Melarrine's sword becomes enchanted with ice power.

"Follow me. We get as close to Neea as we can, fighting our way if we have to. I think we'll have to." He lifted both his sword and staff into the air before him and dramatically swept out into the alley. He spun to his left, lifted his staff...

Melarrine casts Ice Storm on 4 undead. 4 undead die.

"Hurry, we don't have much time. Hit hard, Cure later. Let's go!" Melarrine said, and ran out of sight.

"We better get!" Kevin said, and took off out of the home, following Melarrine with his shield held high.

Amanda and Donny dashed after him, too, and the first thing Donny saw when he entered the shadowy alley was another shadowy alley about forty feet away from them, with at least twenty undead between them and the next dark path they were to take following Melarrine. What did these gnarly undead do, wander every dark corner of Sillia randomly in case they had to fight intruders? It was a game, and this meant more fights. That meant more experience points and possible loot.

Donny got excited.

*

Kevin used Shield Bash every chance he got, crying out, "I bequeath death unto thy undead soul!" each time, but he did so much damage that neither Amanda nor Donny got irritated with him. Donny didn't have to Cure much with Amanda's Throw Knives taking the undead down, and Melarrine simply Ice Stormed groups of the gnarly monsters when there were seemingly dozens of them coming around corners at once. Donny was thrilled to Fireball away at the ghastly, eyeless creatures.

The bodies fell so fast that Donny felt like he was walking through an indoor cemetery where all the bodies had come up from the ground.

He felt like a badass at Level 38. They'd plowed through the last eight levels just getting to Neea.

Yes, Kevin was thoroughly enjoying his new Shield move, and Amanda had learned some kind of trick with her joystick where her knives spun when she threw them. They always came back, and she caught them expertly. So much for a sore thumb.

They were at the top hall of the Palace of Sillia, where Melarrine had said Neea would be. Now that all the undead guarding her were annihilated, Donny didn't see her anywhere. He hadn't gotten a glimpse of her the whole time they fought, either.

Had she even been there?

"Wait a minute. Where is she?" Amanda said, sticking a knife in her belt. "You said she'd be here, Melarrine. So. What gives?"

Kevin turned to Melarrine. "Yeah. Where is she?"

He doused his icy sword by running a gloved hand up the blade and sheathed it. "It appears we'll have to do more climbing. Neea is in the roof pit."

"What the hell is a roof pit?" Amanda said.

"A roof pit. I bet those are the dips," Donny told her.

"What dips? You're a dip. We're running out of time." She spun to Melarrine. "Take us to the roof pit or whatever."

"The way the roofs curved in," Donny said. "Didn't you see it?"

"Yes, Donny is right, Amanda," said Melarrine, voice dancing. "The roofs of the structures of Sillia are curved as though giant balls were resting in them. The Elves who designed Sillia liked to recline in their roof pits at night as they smoked."

"Elves smoke?" Amanda asked.

"Some. Access to roof pits is hard to breach. Neea knows we're here and has the advantage of first strike if she's in the roof pit. There's only one way in."

"What's that?" Donny asked.

Melarrine pointed to a dark corner of the room as the last undead body faded. "See?"

There was a hatch in the ceiling, a ladder reaching down to the ground. Only one person at a time could fit through there.

"God," Amanda said. "Isn't there another way?"

Melarrine shook his head. "Not unless you can fly."

"I can fly," said a voice behind them. Donny whirled around and saw Eln floating outside the window at the fourth floor palace room they were looking for Neea in.

"Eln!" Kevin yelled.

"Shh!" Amanda said. "That Neea will hear you."

"Duh. She knows we're here," said Kevin. "She's hiding. We weren't exactly quiet when we killed all those undead."

"Well, no shit she knows we're here. But she didn't know Eln was here until you screamed his name like he's some kind of movie star."

Eln drifted inside through the window and landed before them. He eyed Melarrine with a slight lift of his upper lip, and then said, "I can use Flight to bring you all to the roof pit. But not you." He pointed at Melarrine.

"Me?" Melarrine said. "Why not me? They need me to defeat Neea and take Sillia. Vampire, you must know this. You cannot help them. You cannot stand the taste of Dark Elf blood."

"And, may I ask, how do you know this?" Eln's tall figure imposed on them all, and Donny felt small and insignificant before him.

"Every Elf—Dark, Elf, or half—knows that you fed on Serranti. Every Elf knows you spat out his blood," explained Melarrine.

"And what of this story gives you the impression I cannot feed on all Elves with Dark Elf blood?" Eln smiled wickedly with both fangs dramatically poking out over his lower lip. Melarrine blinked and leaned back.

"Are you gonna fly us, Eln?" asked Kevin. "That'd be awesome. That'd be so awesome."

"I most certainly intend upon it. However, Melarrine is correct. I do not feed on Dark Elf blood. The smell alone makes me gag." He looked down his nose at Melarrine and his fangs disappeared. "I will not assist in your battle against the granddaughter of Serranti, but I will give you advantage where you had none."

"You may not use your demented magic on me," Melarrine said, but he didn't sound angry. Actually, Donny thought, the half-Elf sounded afraid.

"As you wish, and as was my intent, as stated previously," said Eln. "Come, children of Earth. Come to me by the window. Melarrine, you can find your own way, probably up through the hatch long after Don's party has engaged Neea." He smirked.

Kevin ran over to him. "Thanks, Eln. How did you know we were here?"

Eln bent his neck and looked way down at Kevin the Dwarf. "I'm keeping an eye on my human. And his companions."

"'Cause you want to get back to Earth, right? You're so cool, Eln," said Kevin. "We'll get you back to Earth."

Eln nodded once at Kevin. "I always feel cool. It's part of being dead. Come, come."

Donny and Amanda walked to the window.

"Are you ready? Have your weapons prepared. Have your spells and abilities already in action when I drop you in the roof pit. Neea is in the center. She is alone, watching the hatch expectantly. I will drop you behind her. And you," he said to Melarrine. "You can figure when time is convenient for you to scramble up the hatch ladder at your leisure."

"Ready," Donny said. "Thanks, Eln."

"You are most welcome, Don. Most welcome."

Eln casts Flight. Donny's party take flight.

Donny rose up in the air and out of the window, with Kevin and Amanda following. He had no control over where he went in midair.

He looked down and his heart skipped. If Eln somehow dropped them, they'd be piles of mush. The dark stone road below the palace had to be fifty feet away.

Kevin must have looked down, too, because he said, "Whoa, Eln. Be careful, would ya?"

"I always take the utmost care," Eln said from just above them. "Prepare. We go now."

Donny got his Fireball ready in his menu, thumb hovering over the button on his joystick.

Up they went, and then Donny saw the roof pit of the palace room they'd been in moments ago. In the center of the dipping roof stood Neea. She had pinkish-white, wavy hair past her shoulders, dark blue skin and pure white eyes without pupils, like Lale's eyes had been just light. She wore leather armor. Her chest piece was a tight vest with three daggers in each of three pockets lining the black leather. She had on a tattered, flowing black leather skirt that swirled around her knees and black leather, thigh-high boots as she spun to face them. Eln had dropped them, and she'd heard.

"She's a rogue," said Amanda. "Dark Elf Rogue, level 40. Highest stat is Agility at—"

"You wretched Earthlings!" she cried out, and held her hand out to Donny, pointing. "I know what you are, Donny of Earth. You would not be able to stop him, and you certainly will not stop me. Now, die at my hand!"

Neea Stabs Donny.

"Ow!" Donny yelled. That took some damage.

He retaliated instantly with a Fireball, knocking some HP off of her.

Amanda uses Throw Knives on Neea. Neea takes 99 damage and is stunned for three seconds.

Then, Amanda, being her tough self, caught her knives in one hand as Donny Cured himself. He remembered what Asope had said about always curing himself in case he needed to resurrect Kevin or Amanda.

Neea used a move called Slash on Kevin just after he used Savior on her, and it took 60 damage off him. Donny Cured Kevin immediately. Amanda Triple Shotted her from the other side of the roof pit, taking her attention off of Kevin, and Neea threw her own three blades at Amanda with a move called Night Blades, taking her health down by 100. Donny hastily Cured Amanda. Neea spun on Donny with a wicked grin, all three daggers in her hands glowing violet.

"Damn!" hollered Kevin.

Kevin becomes Savior. Neea is enraged at Kevin.

"Sorry, Don. Got it now."

Neea uses Speed and Slash on Kevin.

Kevin dies.

"Holy shit!" yelled Amanda. "Where the hell is Melarrine?"

Donny Cured himself twice.

Amanda and Neea went at it, knives shining in the moonlight. Amanda did good damage, but not as much as Neea did to her. Donny kept the Cures up, and at first chance...

Donny Resurrects Kevin.

Kevin comes back to life with 120HP.

Kevin's fallen Dwarf form reanimated, floated up in the air in a white glow, and he slowly lowered to the roof pit floor. "Yeah! Thanks, Don! Now, beseech heaven from my wrath, Neea, Dark Elf."

Neea Slashes at Kevin. Kevin takes 83 damage.

Donny wasn't sure if he should Cure himself or Kevin. If Kevin took another hit... well, he'd be dead again. But so would Donny if he took that next hit.

"She has 510HP left!" Amanda called out as she darted around the edges of the roof pit after throwing knives at the Dark Elf rogue, doing 98 damage.

Donny casts Cure on Donny. Donny gains 78HP.

Neea took her attention off Amanda and Kevin, and Stabbed Donny for some bad damage.

"Cure me," Kevin yelled. "I'll get her off you guys."

Donny did as he was told, curing Kevin for 91HP.

Kevin eats Pork Cheek Pie. Kevin has +20 Defense and +10 Strength.

Neea Slashed Kevin, but it didn't hit him nearly as hard as the other times she'd laid into him.

Donny casts Cure on Donny. Donny gains 76HP.

Donny couldn't wait to see how hard Kevin hit after that pie. He took a ton less damage from Neea's hit.

Kevin becomes Savior. Neea is enraged at Kevin.

Neea tried stabbing Kevin, but again, Kevin only took about 30 damage.

Kevin uses Shield Bash on Neea. Neea takes 99 damage.

"Yes!" Donny cried out.

Amanda used Triple Shot as she balanced on the edge of the roof pit, out of Neea's slashing range, doing great damage. Was it Donny's imagination, or was she hitting harder?

Donny almost forgot. Kevin had to be really low on HP.

Donny casts Cure on Kevin. Kevin gains 79HP.

"Finish her, Kevin!" Amanda called out as she dodged behind Kevin.

Neea Stabbed Kevin, but Kevin Blocked, deflecting the damage.

Amanda uses Triple Shot on Neea. Neea takes 102 damage.

This was it. Donny knew it. He grinned under all his wires, goggles and headphones.

Donny casts Fireball on Neea.

Neea dies.

The twisted Dark Elf burned up and fell over, defeated.

"Oh, we did it!" Kevin yelled. "We did it! Great Fireball, Don. We're a great team!"

Amanda put her bow in her arrow sheath and wiped her digital brow. "Whew, that was so fun!"

"No kidding," said Donny. He felt proud that he'd landed the finishing blow on Neea.

"Very well done, well done," said Melarrine. Donny turned to the hatch door in the far left corner of the roof pit. Melarrine climbed out and into the roof pit as he spoke.

"Where the hell were you, Melarrine?" Amanda demanded.

"It doesn't matter, Amanda. We got her good. Yeah, we sure as shit did," Kevin said.

"Watch your language," Amanda told him, and then turned her attention back to Melarrine. "So?"

"More came. Into the room below. They were Dark Elves, not undead. I was delayed, but I conquered them. So worried about the three of you, I was. But, I had no reason to worry. You have expert skills. Yes, you have mastery. Very good, very good," Melarrine said as he stood tall and waved his icy sword at them. "You have defeated Neea. Now, you must get the Onyx Charm from her neck before she fades. That is how she commands the undead."

"Wait a goddamn minute," Amanda said to Melarrine. "I didn't hear anything from below."

Donny went to Neea's fallen, crispy body and saw a silver necklace around Neea's dead neck. In the silver of the necklace's pendant a black, shiny stone was set, and it glowed a soft violet.

"Go. Go look down through the hatch. You'll see the bodies which haven't yet faded. Go, see, young Elf." Melarrine pointed at the hatch, imploring Amanda to witness what he said he'd been doing while they fought Neea.

Donny looked away as Amanda dashed to the hatch. He wondered why she had to be suspicious all the time. The game wouldn't have them ally for every big fight, geez. He bent over Neea's body and yanked the Onyx Charm off her neck just as she faded away.

"I got it!"

"There aren't any bodies, Melarrine," Amanda told him. "I don't believe you."

"Amanda, come on. We did it on our own. We probably had to as part of the quest," Donny explained to her, but she kept her arms folded as she glared at Melarrine, sticking out her bountiful Elven bust, too. Donny covered a grin, even though she wouldn't see it with her goggles on. She was such a poser.

Donny tied the leather rope of the Onyx Charm back together and looped the necklace over his head. It hung at mid-chest and glowed, as though waiting for something.

Melarrine walked away from Amanda, approaching Donny. "Yes, that's it. You have it. Neea made that with the help of an Orcish shaman. Powerful one, from Pariss. Kleemop is his name. You don't want him to target you, no." His voice sang like a lullaby to Donny. "Yes, you have it right. You wear it like that. It responds to your magic. See the pulse of the glow? You have the magic to contain the city of Sillia now. Look," he said, gazing over the edge of the roof pit and down into the streets far below. "Look, you see. The Dark Elves. They feel the power of the Onyx Amulet. They flee. Look."

Donny did. Amanda and Kevin joined him. Dark Elves ran through the streets below in droves, heading for the main gate at the back of the cliff. They'd already gotten the enormous stone gate open, and were pouring out of the city like it was on fire.

"Whoa," said Kevin. "We did that?"

"Yes, oh, yes," Melarrine said. "You did that. Kevin, the moment Donny burned Neea to death, the amulet became his property. That is how it changes hands. That is how it works. It can be given, or it can be taken in this way. Kleemop brought the Onyx Amulet back from a shaman journey to the lower world, gave it to Serranti. Serranti gifted it to his great-granddaughter, Neea. She has resented him. Always, always. Serranti's weakness is his direct lineage. You will see. Not all of them have the same affection back toward him, and certainly not Neea. No." He gazed over the edge of the roof pit, and then stepped back.

Kevin turned to Melarrine. "So, what does the Onyx Amulet do, exactly? How did all them Dark Elves know to run away? And why are they? And why didn't we see any Dark Elves when we were coming here? I mean, there's a ton of them leaving. We just fought undead. What does the Onyx Amulet do?"

"Yeah, Melarrine, what the hell does it do and how do you know all this?" Amanda added, hands on hips.

"Maybe you do not understand. All half-Elves come from Serranti. Lale, you know him. You've spoken with him. He gave you the quest to take Sillia. I know. Lale and Serranti's first trueborn Dark Elf daughter fell in love thousands of years ago and kept it secret. But their offspring were discovered. Serranti's weakness. You'll see what I mean. Serranti made the Vople Nole'on Alliance. It said that the half-Elves could live. Yes, live in Pariss. But, he made law that they were not free, not until the third generation of half-Elves. A third-generation half-Elf is given freedom, but not the others." Melarrine pushed his long, long hair away from his face as a breeze picked up.

"Asope," said Donny.

"Yes, Asope is third-generation half-Elf."

"What are you?" asked Donny.

"I am first-generation half-Elf. You know what that means. You've already wondered. I can tell."

Donny cocked his head. "You're a slave, or you were and you ran away."

Kevin laughed. "Who wouldn't? You're not so bad, Melarrine. Hey, thanks for taking care of the Dark Elves in the room under us."

"I'm still not sure he did," Amanda said to Kevin. She turned to Melarrine, who remained expressionless under her scrutiny. "Well, which is it? Slave or escapee? And what about this Onyx Amulet?"

"I escaped. I certainly did, and you would have, too. It was difficult. I will never have true freedom until Serranti loses power."

"And the amulet?" Amanda said.

"The Onyx Amulet, as I said, is from the lower world. The undead are also from the lower world. The Onyx Amulet will have you, Donny, in control of what the undead do, and you must now use the Onyx Amulet to make the undead hold the city until Elves can come and claim it for good. Then, you will give the Elf Lale deems worthy of holding Sillia the Onyx Amulet, and he or she will control the undead. Kleemop warned of this. This is how I knew to take the amulet." The crystal in the top of his staff fluctuated with white light, then faded to a gentle hue.

"What exactly did this Kleemop warn of, Melarrine?" Amanda asked, frowning at him.

"He warned Serranti that the Onyx Amulet could be taken, that there was a weakness with its power over the undead. It is the only thing that controls them. Nothing else controls them in this world." Melarrine tilted his head at Amanda. "You do not trust me. I understand. It is hard to trust with so many lies everywhere you turn. My life has been finding truths between lies."

"And what have you found out? What else do you know? Why are you even helping us?" Amanda asked, glaring at Melarrine. Nope, she didn't like him at all. Still, she stuck her chest out. *She must like him a little,* Donny thought.

Melarrine shook his head. "Do not take me the wrong way. See what I did? I assisted you. I assist the Elves. You can see this clearly by my actions, young Elf." He looked at Donny. "You surely see it."

"Yeah, of course, Melarrine. I see it. So. Uh, okay. Uh. How do I use the Onyx Amulet and control the undead?"

"You *will* it. You use your magic."

Amanda looked at Donny. "Really? Like, look in your menu and see if you can just select to use it or something."

"Yeah," Donny said. "Good idea."

Lo and behold, there was an option in the menu to "use" the Onyx Amulet, so without a thought, Donny selected the option.

The amulet around his neck pulsed with a black light aura, and Donny heard cries from below.

"What's that? What's all the screaming for?" Kevin asked, doing his Dwarf warrior squat at the edge of the roof pit, looking down. "I don't see nothing."

"That is the undead attacking the Dark Elves who have not yet made it out of Sillia. Yes, you did it, Donny. You have claimed Sillia for the Elves. They will reward you greatly." He smiled. Donny realized Melarrine had not once smiled until just then. "Now, I must go. I am still hunted. You wait here until the Elves arrive. They most likely will come on the Diamond Dragon within the hour. Hold the city, hold it well. I take my leave. The undead of the Marion Jungle beyond Sillia will now be after the Dark Elves, and will no longer attack Elves. Or you. Any of you. Thank you, Donny." He turned to Kevin and Amanda. "Thank you, Amanda and Kevin. You fought bravely. You have done well with this part of the quest."

"What do we do now?" Kevin asked. "I mean, do we just wait or something?"

"Yes, wait. Wait until the new leader of Sillia arrives, and give that Elf the Onyx Amulet. The Elves will not destroy the undead, for now they are sentient. They are life. Elves treat life with respect. They will teach the undead the ways of Elves. Now, I must go before they arrive."

"Why?" Amanda asked.

"Because, because I am always in danger, and I do not ever know who to trust."

"Then why did you trust us?" Amanda asked. "Why didn't you just get the Onyx Amulet yourself?"

"Oh, I could not have done that alone. I knew Lale had given your party this quest. I heard it on the wind."

"Heard it on the wind. That's your pipeline?" Amanda said.

"Pipeline? I know not of a line of pipes. I do have some I trust, and they keep me in the know. I go now. Stay safe." He spun around and walked quickly toward the roof pit's hatch.

"Wait," Amanda called out to him. "Is there a Save Point fountain around here?"

"Amanda, no! It's just getting good!" Kevin said. "Well, I mean, it's all awesome, but come on."

Donny shook his head, knowing it was no use.

Melarrine spoke over his shoulder as he climbed through the hatch. "Yes, in this palace, on the bottom floor in a room west of the entrance. I take my leave." He disappeared through the hatch.

"Well, I guess… we go," said Donny.

"Come on, guys, it feels like we've been playing this for three days straight. I have stuff to do, and I have to pee again," Amanda said.

"How do you have to pee? You haven't even drunk anything," said Kevin.

"Shut up, goon. Let's go."

CHAPTER 7

"God!" Amanda moaned and bent her thumb all around. "That's just ridiculous. How the hell can you play all day like that, Donny? Jesus. Mom will be home any sec. Come on, I have to get ready."

Kevin examined his goggles like they were artifacts from the future. "What in the world could you hafta do that's better than this? Huh?"

Amanda snatched the goggles out of Kevin's hands. "You're going to mess them up. Just put them to the side. Quit. Quit trying to grab them. Donny, he's worse than you. No wonder I have such a dork for a brother. Your friends are dorkier than you." She tucked everyone's goggles and headphones neatly next to the TV on the floor.

"Why you even putting them by the TV?" Kevin said. "We don't use the TV at all."

"Shut up. Donny, go upstairs and put the oven on 350. I'll throw in last night's meatloaf," Amanda said, giving Kevin a look.

"Sure thing," Donny said and got up. He stretched out his stiff back. His own thumb ached a little bit.

"I'll go with you, Don. Man, we musta played for a hundred hours and I'm not even tired."

"Don't you have to be home or something?" Amanda asked Kevin. "Like, aren't your parents going to freak that you've been gone all freaking day?"

"They don't care what I do." He grinned. "I'm my own man."

"More like your own pube. I'll take you home. With my luck, you live in the suburbs."

"No," Kevin said, eyes wide. "I—I gotta stay."

"Why?" Hands on hips. Donny noticed she wasn't sticking out her chest.

"Because of Quest."

"We're done playing that game for the day. Come on. Donny, do the oven, put in dinner when its preheated."

"No! Come on. What you gotta do, Amanda? What's better than Quest?" Kevin pleaded.

She shrugged and wrapped up the cable for the game's microphone. "Just Killer coming over. We're going to run through some songs I wrote."

Donny turned on the stairs. "How's he doing that without his drums?"

Amanda threw eyeball knives at Donny. "He just is. Go."

"I can't believe you'd quit Quest for a few hours of that," Kevin complained, standing up from where he'd stayed sitting on the floor as though they would start playing again any minute.

"You like him," Donny said.

"Shut up. It's just stupid Killer. I don't like anyone."

"You like Killer. You like a guy who goes by the name Killer," Donny said and laughed.

Kevin joined in with a chuckle. "That is pretty funny. Killer. Like he's ever killed anybody."

"Shut up, you freaking goons," Amanda said, and punched Kevin's shoulder.

"Ow!"

Amanda pulled back like she was going to punch him again, but they heard their mother from upstairs call down.

"I'm home, kids! Amanda, I'll get dinner going, don't worry about it. Nice to see you two doing something together down there. Pac-Man?"

Amanda and Donny stared at each other, and then Donny looked up at his mother standing in the basement doorway. He hadn't even seen her open the door. She looked tired, but she smiled. He opened his mouth to answer, to tell his mom about Quest.

"Yeah, Mom," Amanda called up to her. "It's wicked."

"That's nice. You two keep going, then. I'll make something special," she called down, smiling at Donny, and then she closed the basement door.

"Why did you say that?" Donny asked her.

"Look," Amanda told him. "Let's not tell Mom about this Quest game. Actually, let's not tell anyone."

"Why not?" Donny said.

"Yeah," Kevin added. "Why?"

She shrugged and looked at the game's mess of cables by the TV. "It's... not right. I just think we should keep it to ourselves. And Donny, don't say anything to Mom about those damn bullies, either."

"I haven't yet," Donny said. "I know better, believe me."

Amanda looked up at him. He hadn't moved from the stairs. "Good. We'll take care of them. Mom doesn't need to know anything that reminds her of damn Dad."

"They know," Kevin said quietly.

"What?" Amanda said, turning to him.

Donny came back down the stairs.

"Brian Boyd and them. They saw us playing Quest. They know about the game. Well, they know something, anyway."

Amanda slapped her forehead. "Dammit. They do. Shit." She looked back at the 3D controller mess. "We have to hide all this."

"Why don't you tell that Killer guy not to come over and we'll play more?" Kevin said.

"I have to see Killer," Amanda said.

"But, why? Like, don't you guys have practice? Isn't that for learning new songs? And Don said he won't even have his drums. Is Don right and you just like him?" Kevin said.

"Shut up, shut up! You two are so freaking nosey. It'll take Mom an hour if she's cooking something nice, and Killer should be here at nine. I have just enough time to take you home, Kevin." Amanda scooped up the pile of wires, goggles and headphones, stashing the mic under her arm. "I'm going to put this in my trunk. Donny, grab the game. Put it in the box. Bring it. You're coming with me to drop off Kevin."

"No! Amanda, please. I can eat with you. You can call Killer and tell him you're busy. With the time difference in Quest, we could finish the game by midnight," Kevin pleaded. "Come on."

"What's the hurry?" Amanda asked. "Weird dude at the weird shop said you have five days."

"But the Elves will be in Sillia by now," Kevin said. "We have to get the amulet to them. Right, Don?"

"Yeah, that's right. Amanda?" Donny said, but he knew it was useless. If Amanda liked Killer all of a sudden, there was nothing that would keep her from seeing him tonight.

"It's a freaking game. It'll be at the same spot when we play again. Idiots."

Kevin looked at Donny. "Don? Maybe you and me can play while Killer is here? Yeah?"

Amanda didn't let Donny answer. "No. You play with me."

Donny agreed with her but was curious. "So, you're into it?"

She glared down at him. "Of course I'm into it. You're an idiot if you think I'm not. It's a crazy game. I mean, what is it, right?"

Donny relaxed. He knew he couldn't play it without her.

"So, if you want to play it, and Donny wants to play it, and I want to play it, and we all hafta play it together, can I spend the night? That way, after Killer leaves, we can play again. All night, right, Don? Amanda?" He looked back and forth at them, waiting for an answer.

Donny didn't want Kevin spending the night at his house. If people at school found out Kevin spent a Saturday night with him, he'd have more than Brian and company picking on him. But he desperately wanted to play more Quest, more than anything in the world. "Well..."

"I don't even hafta come up for your dinner. Your mom doesn't even hafta know I'm here! I can be so quiet. I'll even hide in the closet if you want."

Donny rolled his eyes. "Amanda, if he stays, will you play more? Tonight, after Killer leaves?" The temptation of more Quest tonight outweighed his fear of being made fun of for hanging out with Kevin, the dorkiest kid in school. Besides, how would anyone find out? "Kevin, just don't tell anyone you stayed here."

"Why not?"

Donny thought fast. "Because then they'd somehow figure out about Quest. We have to keep it a secret, remember?" He felt bad. He was being a bully like Brian and them, in a way. "Why don't you come up for dinner? Meet Mom?"

"Won't she be mad I'm here?"

"Of course not. Why would she?" Donny asked.

Kevin shrugged with a big grin. "My dad would be pissed if I had someone over and didn't ask first. But I guess your mom's cool, huh, Don? I can't wait. I bet your mom's a great cook. I'm starving."

Amanda put the game stuff in the closet and covered it up with a blanket. "Donny, put the game under here. Come on, let's help Mom. She'll get all giddy thinking we actually got along for a day. Let's go make her happy for once." She half-grinned at Donny. "And she'll flip that you have a friend over." She turned to Kevin. "Donny doesn't have any friends."

"Yes, I do!"

"Not any that come over here. Come on, let's go."

*

"You have a great backyard, Don," Kevin said, slurping on the hot chocolate Donny's mom had given them after dinner. Who made that much noise drinking something? "My mom never makes me hot chocolate. You're lucky. Mom just gives me ice cream after dinner. You got pie and hot chocolate. You're so lucky." Slurp.

"Yeah, Mom's pretty cool." Donny looked out over the dark yard, full of dead grass from the cold winter. Amanda blared the beginning of London Dungeon by the Misfits from her room, where she and Killer were supposed to be practicing band songs.

"That song is pretty cool. Don't know how your sis is supposta get any music learning done with that loud music," Kevin said between loud sips.

Donny's nose ran from the hot chocolate steam in the cold night air. Sure, he had thought he'd be deep into hour ten of Pac-Man by this time today, but what actually had happened was so much cooler. Quest—what a game. There wasn't anything in the world like it, was there? "I don't think they're practicing music, Kevin."

"What are they—oh. Oh, yeah. You said she liked Killer. Man, that's a stupid name. I mean, it's like every town has at least three punk rockers named Killer, right, Don?" Kevin put his cup down on the step next to him. "What is it, nine-thirty? When do you think they'll be done? I mean, we could go play another Atari game if you want, but I don't think I want to play another Atari game ever again after Quest."

"Yeah, me neither."

"Amanda's cool, though. I thought she'd be stuck up. She's rude for sure, but I get it. It's part of her persona. Like, she's in a band and all. She's supposta be all tough, cuss a lot. It's her image. Your image is important, don't you think? I think I've got an okay image. Nobody messes with me. Hey, think your mom will make me more hot chocolate?"

"Shouldn't you call your mom and let her know you're spending the night?" Donny just thought of it. If he had been gone all day, and planned on spending the night somewhere—not that it ever, ever happened—his mother would kill him if he didn't call. Kevin hadn't called his parents once.

"Oh, yeah. I totally forgot. Mom'll be okay with it. My parents love it when I'm not home. They said so." He rubbed chocolate off his lips and chin. Donny was glad he didn't have to tell the kid it was there. "I can't wait to play more Quest."

"Spending the night with your boyfriend, Donny?" Brian's voice came from the darkness to the right. Donny's head snapped to that direction and his body stiffened. "Atari game named Quest you're playing? Is that a new way of saying making out with your boyfriend?"

Out of the nothingness of a moonless March night, Brian, Duff, and Ernie appeared, walking through Donny's backyard toward them. Ernie carried a steel baseball bat, tapping the barrel in his left hand over and over with a heavy, fleshy thud each time.

Both Donny and Kevin stood up. "Crap," Kevin muttered.

"Get out of my yard," Donny told them, but his voice shook. He kept it down. He didn't want his mother to hear them. Not that she'd be able to over Amanda's music, but just in case.

"What the hell you faggots doing in your basement, Donny?" Brian asked. They were just feet away, and Ernie now swung the baseball bat by his leg.

"What's all them wires? What's them glasses for?" asked Duff. God, he was tall. His fists, balled up and ready for action, looked like sledgehammers.

Kevin jumped down the steps and got in Duff's face. "None of your business, stinking dog."

The three of them laughed as Duff shoved Kevin to the ground with little effort. "Oh, you're so mean, little faggot," said Brian. "Your mother wash out your faggot mouth with soap too much and you forgot how to talk like a man?"

"Nah, he's just a little girl," said Ernie.

"That must be why you like him so much, Donny," said Brian, smirking. "What the hell are you three doing down there? Your sister like watching faggots rub their fat ones together? She's a freak. She probably does."

Kevin was already back up and now got in Brian's personal space. "You don't talk about her like that. Take it back or I'll punch you in the face."

Brian looked down at short, fat Kevin giving it his all. Donny was terrified. "Go ahead. Try." He said it so quietly that Donny barely heard it over Danzig's unholy voice. Brian's eyes were like snake eyes, assessing when to strike.

Kevin pulled back his right arm, ready to go for it, but Duff grabbed his elbow and yanked his arm behind his back. "Tell Brian you're sorry," he said as Kevin cried out in pain. Duff had Kevin's arm jacked up behind his back, bent, and was putting the pressure on. Duff had done that to Donny a couple times before, and it was nothing to joke about.

"Leave him alone!" Donny yelled.

Make sure your face is clean now... The song spilled out to the night air.

Duff kept the pressure on as Brian smiled at Donny. "Ask nicely. Ask... no, say, 'I love to suck fat boy's little twig all night,' and then Duff'll think about letting him go."

All the corpses here are clean, boy...

"Ohhhh, that hurts," Kevin moaned, his entire face and neck bright red in the darkness.

Donny was furious, yet frightened. "Just stop, okay?"

"We'll stop, maybe, if you tell us what you're doing in the basement," said Brian, walking up to the bottom of the porch steps, never taking his eyes off Donny. "With the new Atari game? Quest?"

Kevin kept making gagging noises but somehow managed to get out, "Don't you do it, Don, ow, don't do it!"

"Shut up, faggot," said Duff as he twisted Kevin's arm a little, making the kid squeal.

"Stop!" Donny burst out. He couldn't stand watching it.

"Tell me what you got down there."

Ain't no mystery why I'm in misery in hell...

Donny gritted his teeth and saw everything in shades of deep maroon, and then he launched himself at Brian.

But he didn't make it.

Ernie swung the bat. It hit Donny full-force in the chest, knocking the very breath out of him and stopping his impulsive, attempted attack on Brian.

Here's hoping you're swell...

Donny fell on his face on the freezing ground and gasped for air, loud, heaving groans coming from him with every struggling breath. He heard Kevin cry out in desperate pain. Duff must be about to break his arm.

Here's hoping you're swell...

The bat came down on Donny's lower back, flattening him on the grass. Pain shot through his skeletal system like all his bones were shattering. It hurt so much that Donny couldn't even scream from it. He had no more breath; he had no sight because Brian had planted his foot on the back of Donny's head and pressed his face into the dirt with all his weight. Was he standing on Donny's head?

Here's hoping you're swell...

Through his haze of insane pain and shock and fear, Donny heard the three of them laughing like this was the funniest thing any of them had ever seen or done. Their laughter had a ghoulish edge to it. They could be evil spirits of the dead come to bring Donny and Kevin over to their side. Donny had no idea what Brian was capable of if he got angry enough.

"London Dungeon" ended, and Minor Threat's "Filler" pounded out through the yard from Amanda's room. Donny's mother definitely couldn't hear Brian and the guys beating the shit out of them even if Donny wanted her to.

The bat came down again on Donny's ass with a thick *thunk* as Brian took his shoe off Donny's head. His butt burned bad, and the hit kept him down, but he turned his face out of the grass and dirt to look at Kevin. Duff shoved Kevin away from him and down next to Donny as Brian said, "One on the tushie. We're just trying to prevent faggots from faggoting comfortably. You're bottom tonight, fat boy."

You're full of shit, Minor Threat belted out.

"Uhhhhh…" Kevin groaned, not lifting his head. All Donny could see of him was his shoulders and the back of his head.

"Look how cute them is, Bri," said Duff. "They look like they in love for real."

"I'm sure they are," Brian said. "Hey, faggots. Have a romantic night tonight. We'll be back. You didn't tell us what's in your basement and we're gonna find out."

"Buh-bye," called out Ernie as the three swaggered into the black night.

The Minor Threat song ended before it seemed to play, and The Damned started up. Through the shock and pain, Donny cursed Amanda's mixtape for making this beatdown more terrifying.

He slowly sat up. His butt pounded with pain instantly and he leaned onto his left hip, watching Kevin. "Hey, you alright? Your arm?"

Kevin pushed himself up with his good arm and flipped over, sitting up and bending over his knees. "How's a jerk gonna kick you in the shin when he's got you like that, huh?" he muttered. "Yeah, I'm alright. I've had worse. You okay, Don?"

Donny wasn't okay. Not in the least. He still hurt too much to stand up. "Yeah, I'll be fine."

"That bat couldn't have felt good, Don. Just sayin'."

"It was a bitch."

"We ain't no faggots."

Donny shook his head, and then chuckled. Name-calling was the least of his worries, but apparently Kevin was insulted. "They're just being jerkheads. Don't sweat it."

"Still," Kevin said, moving his twisted arm back and forth while wincing. "I don't like it. We gotta stop them before they start next time. We'll have a plan next time."

"There won't be a next time."

Kevin dropped his arm and his widening eyes focused on Donny. "You gonna get them, Don? You got a plan?"

"No, that's not what I meant." He wished he had a plan. "I mean, you won't be around next time."

"What do you mean, I won't be around? I'll be here for five days. Well, after school, anyway." He cocked his head. "Right, Don?"

"Yeah, but that's it. After that, no. And we'll probably be done by morning if my stupid sister will ever get done sucking that drummer's face." Donny spit it out, furious, not thinking about how it would make Kevin feel.

"Oh, oh, okay," Kevin said quietly. "I knew that. Right."

Donny realized then how mean it had sounded, but he didn't care. Kevin wasn't his friend. They were just playing Quest until it was over. "Let's get inside. They might come back."

"Sure, sure. Whatever you want to do, Don. Whatever." Kevin got up without a sound, watching as Donny struggled to his feet. "You need help there?"

"No."

"Okay, just asking. You don't have to be all whatever about it."

Donny knew he'd hurt Kevin's feelings by the tone of the kid's voice. *Dammit,* he thought. He'd let those assholes get to him. It made him be mean to Kevin, who had tried to stand up for him. Donny felt like a jerk.

"Let's just go inside," he told Kevin once he was standing steady. He kept a death grip on the porch railing as he climbed the steps to the backdoor. God, his butt and chest and head and back ached.

"You don't look too good," Kevin said. "You got dirt all over your face. Better clean that up before Amanda sees it."

Donny paused with his hand on the doorknob. "What makes you say that?" He was more worried about his mom seeing it.

"She'll send Killer after them. Nobody wants a punk rock drummer named Killer with green Liberty Spikes coming after them. She'd sick him on Brian and them like a dog, and he'd probably kill all three of them. Just sayin'."

Donny hung his head and shook it, eyes closed. "Look, let's get inside and cleaned up before anyone sees us. Nobody ever has to know about it."

"Don, everybody knows Brian's after you. It's why you don't got no friends. Everybody's too scared to be your friend because Brian's told them he'll kick their ass if they talk nice to you. Guess you didn't know that."

"No, I didn't."

"Well, he did and he does, but I don't give a shit."

Donny looked back at Kevin. Kevin offered a small smile. He had dirt on his face, too.

"Thanks, Kevin." Donny smiled back. "You're a nice kid. Nicer than me."

CHAPTER 8

"It seems like certain stats go with certain types of spells or abilities," said Amanda.

They were in the Laranda Flame Swamp in a safe spot outside Laranda, where they'd decided to lie low and wait for Asope to give them their Level 40 moves and spells. It had been thirty minutes, yet no Asope. Donny had thought to ask Amanda what she'd noticed about how stats work, what she might have seen using Insight on everything.

"Like," she continued, "Donny, you cast Cure a lot, and the main stat with that, or, well, the first one listed, at least, if my theory is right. Look, it's like I think the first one listed on the scroll is the stat that you get more credit toward if you use the spell, and is also the stat that makes the spells with that stat listed better, stronger. So, Donny, you cast Cure a lot, and Purpose is that one's main stat, and your Purpose keeps getting higher. Like, your Intellect. It does the same thing. See?"

Donny did see, and said so, adding, "Yeah. What do you mean by stats go with spells?"

She scanned through the weeds of the patch of ground they hid in. "I still don't see any Trolls. It's been, like, ten minutes and not a Troll or one of those flames bursting out of the ground. I picked the perfect place to wait. Magic Elf eyes. Go freaking figure."

"Amanda," Kevin said. "Hey, stick with it."

"Shut up, Dwarf. You don't have magic Dwarf eyes."

"I have a magic appetite. So, you shut up."

"Don't tell me to shut up ever again." She leaned back into their nest, now whispering as though it mattered. "Donny, your Cure and Resurrect both have Purpose as the first listed stat. I think Purpose is kinda like a healing stat. But then your Power of One is also Purpose, but its use is to drain Purpose. So, that's not very healing. Every other one works out to be like that except Purpose. My Agility moves make my Agility higher, and the moves get stronger. Agility has to do with accuracy of my moves, how often they hit right, and how much more often they do higher damage. Like, a lot higher. You know, Donny, like how when you cast Fireball and hit almost 20HP higher, right?"

"Yeah, I get it."

"I'm a little confused," Kevin said. "You just said Purpose isn't like that, so how can stats work like that?"

"God, do you listen? I said that. I said Purpose is different, but the rest work like that. I gave examples. You don't listen. Hello? Can you hear me?" Amanda knocked on his helmet.

Donny tried to stop laughing. He just couldn't.

"Stop it! You're so mean, Amanda," Kevin said, shoving her long arm away from his helmet with his shield. "I get it, I guess."

"Good." She sat straight. "So, there's something about Purpose that's special and different. Get it? This game's design has to do with the Purpose stat."

"Okay," Donny said. "I don't get that."

"Me neither," Kevin added.

"Okay, so. Listen, Kevin. Listen. With your ears. Donny said it earlier before we started playing again. He said it about the Neea fight, that all games have patterns. They do. They absolutely do, but I don't see one better about this game than my Purpose stat theory." She looked at Donny. "We made you party leader, and Howlinowa said you had to be human. Everyone makes a big deal out of you being human. Humans' race-specific ability is Power of One, and it cuts whoever your fighting's Purpose stat in half. That would be a very big deal in Quintarria. Think about it. No humans, and there's something archers have called Insight that would tell every character in the game, supposedly, somehow or another, that humans have this. So, Donny, you're a big deal for being human because you cut anything in combat with you's Purpose stat in half. That's big damage. You really should resurrect some things we kill before they fade every once in a while and build your Purpose stat. It's got something to do with winning this game."

"I want to win Quest," Kevin said. "I'm going to."

"So am I," Donny said with a grin.

"Of course we're going to win. We're going to beat the record. I mean, we'll be done by morning, and the old guy gave us five days. I'm not as pissed at him about the rental crap anymore." She grinned.

"Yeah. It's the best game ever made," Kevin said. "Glad you get it now."

"I get it. I always got it, idiot."

"You just had to teach a drummer named Killer some songs while blaring a punk rock mixtape?" Kevin asked.

"Yeah, and can you believe that stereo Mom got her?" Donny added.

"Shut up. It was important. Now," she lowered her voice again, but stopped. Her eyes moved over their heads.

Donny heard a familiar swooshing sound. That was what he heard the last time Asope teleported. Was that Asope landing from a teleport?

He turned around.

Asope parted the long weeds and swamp grass, entering their nest. "You found the only place in the Laranda Flame Swamp where there are neither fire spouts nor Trolls."

"We've been waiting for you, Asope," Kevin said. "Amanda thinks she's so special because she has magic Elf eyes and found this spot."

Asope nodded at Amanda, who stood up and brushed herself off, even though she had nothing on her. "Elves have many magics." He smiled at Kevin. "As do Dwarves, but different kinds. Have you tried mining in Quintarria yet?"

"Why would I mine? There's nothing to spend the money on if I mined something and sold it."

"Ah," said Asope. "The Dwarves have great underground cities where there is much trade. You do think like a Dwarf. Dwarves have the best economy. An open market."

"What, would I have magic Dwarf eyes if I mined? Could I see diamonds and stuff?"

"You'd see something," said Asope. He gestured around at us. "I cannot stay long. Even now, Marrinoff speeds to you to assist in taking Laranda. The Chimera holds Laranda. It is a wicked, three-headed beast. You have to kill it to get to the Key of Laranda, which is bound with a magical chain around the Chimera's neck. Marrinoff the Elf will help you defeat the Chimera."

"What do we do with the Key of Laranda?" Donny asked. "What does it unlock?"

"Very good question," Asope said. "It unlocks the Throne Room of Laranda."

"So, uh, what's in the Throne Room of Laranda?" Donny said.

"Within lies, on the throne, the Troll Stone, which you, Donny, must melt with fire. Nothing but fire from a Wizard will destroy it, and then the Trolls will also burn up and be gone. Marrinoff will deal with the Dark Elves left, if there are any."

"So, that's our next quest?" Kevin said.

"Yes, it is. You are most perceptive. Now, I will assign your new spells and moves.

"Amanda, to you I give Invisibility, which have the stat attributes Agility and Charm. You will now be able to become invisible to your opponents."

"Asope, thanks, but we're fighting Trolls. Their race-specific makes it so they can see through that." Donny noticed she was sticking her chest out again, but unlike with Melarrine, she smiled. She didn't look pissed off for once.

Asope smiled back and tossed his hair. "I think you, Amanda, will find ways around that." He turned to Kevin. "To you, I grant the ability

Demolish Foe. With this ability, you can instantly slice in half any foe that attacks you first and is a lower level."

"So, he dies? Like, right away?"

"Yes, Kevin," Asope said.

"You cut him in half. What do you think?" Amanda said.

"Cool. I gotta do it now." Kevin turned toward the swamp.

"No, wait," Donny said. "I gotta get mine."

"Okay, okay."

"Also, Kevin, look for the feasting table in Laranda's palace. You might find food for your quest. Helpful."

"Oh, man. I haven't eaten the pie yet. It sounds so good."

"Idiot. It's not real," Amanda said.

Asope turned to Donny. "To you, Donny, I grant Unholy Storm. You can call upon an army of Wizard ancestors to attack one or many foes and deal damage. This is purposeful."

"See?" Amanda hissed. "Purposeful. It's about Purpose." She faced Asope again with that same smile, like she knew something about him and liked what she had heard.

Donny wondered if his sister was a slut. She had just been "practicing music" with Killer a few hours ago, and now she was flirting with a game character. A game character who seemed to like it, because Donny saw rows of gold earrings every time he and Amanda talked.

"Asope," Amanda said. "What's up with the stat Purpose?"

"That is, perhaps, better explained by Marrinoff, who should be here any moment. I must take my leave. I have stayed away from Pariss too long. Notice of my absences must not be taken. Surely you understand, Amanda."

"Yeah, yeah. I get it."

"Thank you. I must part. Goodbye for now. I'll see you at Level 50, if not sooner. I certainly hope it's sooner." He was talking to all of them, but he said the last part to Amanda. Donny was going to be sick.

Asope stepped out of their nest, turned his back to them, and *whoosh!*

Asope Teleports.

"I gotta look at my stat scroll. Guys, look at your stat scrolls," Kevin said, sounding like he was so excited he was about to jump out of his armor and streak through Laranda Flame Swamp.

Donny did as he was told.

Donny—Human—Wizard—Level 40
Strength: 38
Defense: 32
Agility: 30
Intellect: 46
Charm: 37
Purpose: 47
Hit Points (Maximum Health): ***310/310HP***
Power of One (Race Specific)—Purpose
Storm Rage (Class Specific)—Strength, Intellect
Fireball—Strength, Intellect
Cure—Purpose, Intellect
Resurrect—Purpose, Intellect
Unholy Storm—Intellect, Strength

"Hey, my Unholy Storm has Intellect, and then Strength listed. Isn't that cool? My strength is so low," Donny said.

"Strength is always good to have leveled high in your stats," said a quiet voice very close to Donny. A male voice, sonorous, like a spring breeze through a mountain forest's treetops.

He turned to see who it was, already assuming it was Marrinoff, and he was right.

Marrinoff was so tall that Donny had to crane his neck back to see his face. He had long, flowing blonde hair, shining silver armor made of steel and red leather, and wore an enormous bow on his back. Was he an archer like Amanda? He had a sharp, angular face, and his eyes were bright blue, and seemed to know everything about them as he examined them one by one. Nobody said anything, waiting for the imposing Elf to speak first. Even Amanda was silent.

"I've come to help you with the Chimera, but we don't have much time. Even now, Serranti looks for the three of you. Donny, Human Mage, he knows about you. He knows what you've come to do." He peered deep into Donny's soul.

"What's he come to do?" Kevin asked.

Good question, Donny thought. This sounded to him like he was about to find out how to beat the game.

"He's something called an Elder Elf Watcher," Amanda said quietly. "Level 72. Strange sounding spells and abilities. His Defense is through the roof. It's 89. Wow."

"Yes, I've had to defend myself throughout the ages, and later, I've had to defend the Elves. Now I defend you. We shall go to Laranda as soon as possible, but first, I must explain to you about the Life Plant. Taking Laranda will not be easy. There will be much bloodshed, and hopefully not ours. You must understand what you are fighting for."

"Finally, someone telling us about the Life Plant," said Kevin. "It's about time." Apparently, Marrinoff's imposing persona's impression had worn off on Kevin.

"Yes," said Marrinoff, staring at Kevin. "You must understand what the Life Plant is in order to understand the extent of Serranti's power."

"I'm listening," said Amanda. She folded her leather-clad arms across her chest. Donny noticed she wasn't messing with her knives or arrows. She didn't try to intimidate Marrinoff. Was his sister actually intimidated... by a game character?

He nodded at her. "Then we all agree to waste no time. The Life Plant sustains the life force of Quintarria. Now, I will show you what a Watcher does. I will take you through time to see what I have seen."

"Are you the one Eln told us about?" Donny asked. "The one who could see all through time?"

"Eln might have been speaking of me, yes."

"And you know Eln?" Kevin asked, smiling. "He's just the best."

"Eln and I have spent time together, yes."

"Isn't he cool?" Kevin continued.

"I suppose one could see him that way."

"Well," Amanda said, "show us the Life Plant story."

Marinoff used his power to store and share memories directly into the trio's minds.

Donny couldn't see the Laranda Flame Swamp anymore, but rather he was in a peaceful glade at night. In the glade stood Marrinoff and two other Elves, and they were in a triangle looking down, holding their glowing hands out over a leafy, small plant. It looked like an ordinary house plant, and it also glowed from whatever magic the three Elves seemed to be putting into it. While their hands glowed white, the Life Plant glowed deep blue, so strong that it lit their faces the same hue even though their hands pulsed white.

It was like watching a 3D movie.

Donny heard Marrinoff's voice, but it wasn't coming from the Marrinoff by the Life Plant. It came from all around. "We tended the Life Plant since we came into being. We believe it brought us into being. Three must tend the Life Plant at all times. The Elves learned not only how to tend to the Life Plant to bring the Elves and other creatures of Quintarria harmony, but we imbued Quintarria with its energy, making all life in Quintarria part of the Life Cycle. It is where magic comes from. It is where the natural order is sustained.

"Now, I will take you into the memory of another time."

Donny was in the same glade, but it was twilight and the trees around the glade had grown enormous. The grass around the Life Plant was unkempt. No Elves surrounded it. It still glowed a gentle blue, but not as vividly as the last memory Marrinoff had shown them.

"Lale, the Fire Mage, was at one time a guardian of the Life Plant. He tried to bring new life into Quintarria with the Life Plant's mysterious powers. He brought the Dark Elves into being. They sprung from the Life Plant. A new race was born, and they settled in Quintarria, nothing like they are now. However, one Dark Elf was different."

Donny saw a dark figure walking toward the Life Plant from the forest. He felt terror as the figure came closer to the plant and he could make out its image.

It was a Dark Elf for sure, but it was deformed. His face was wrecked. Blue skin and pointy ears, but hardly any hair. White strands came out from the back of his head and blew around his wretched cheeks. His nose filled most of his face, bending fat and low over a lipless mouth full of chipped and pointed, rotted teeth. His eyes were two tiny black dots, each with a red pinpoint of red light in them. His blue forehead was wide and long, sloping back, and his chin was nonexistent, blending into his thick neck. It was his skin that creeped Donny out most. His blue Dark Elf skin was pockmarked and wrinkled and scarred, but not from acne, age, or war. To Donny, it looked like it could only come from being a horrid creature in his heart.

It had to be Serranti.

"Man, he's ugly," said Kevin from nowhere. Donny couldn't see him, nor Amanda.

"I never thought I'd agree with you on anything, but yeah. Ugg-o," said Amanda's voice.

Marrinoff continued. "Serranti was the first Dark Elf to come from the Life Plant, and he was and still is the most powerful. Quintarria had never seen a Warlock. Not one. Serranti had powers none could understand, much less combat, and he had a purpose in his black heart. He is of destruction, and he is of ends."

Serranti reached the untended Life Plant and lifted his left arm, extending long, way too long, blue and gnarled fingers over the leaves. Where the Elves had seemed to be putting the white glow from their hands into the Life Plant, Serranti sucked the Life Plant's blue light up into his ghastly palm, making it also glow blue. The plant yielded after seeming to fight. Its light pulsed madly and then it steadily fed Serranti as the glow took over his whole body. Donny watched in horror as Serranti became even more deformed and wretched in appearance.

"This is how Serranti tended it himself. Tended the Life Plant after he defeated the Elves tending to it in an attack. He took from it. He did not look this way when he sprung from the Life Plant. No, he looked like a normal Dark Elf. Some of us speculate that his draining the Life Plant also deformed his thinking, because the Dark Elves in general were not like him. We discuss this at length, and cannot find a starting point where Serranti thought to use the Life Plant this way.

"Instead of using the Life Plant for life, he used it for destruction. Here—look."

Now, Donny saw Dark Elves, Trolls, undead, and Orcs running through the lands and killing Elves. It was like a movie montage. It seemed to go on forever.

"I got it, thanks, Marrinoff," said Kevin. "Don't show no Dwarves, okay?"

"I will not show you Dwarves, as you ask."

"Thank you."

"Yeah," Amanda said. "I think that's enough carnage. I'm ready to do some of my own carnage. That Serranti sucks."

"Yes," Marrinoff said, "he does, indeed, suck. He has built a portal. I will show you that."

"Eln said something about a portal," Donny said.

Marinoff took their minds there.

Now, Donny was in the top of a high tower, and in the center of the round room was a black-and-purple pulsing hole. The glowing colors swirled. Lightning shot at its edges.

"Serranti used his powers from the Life Plant to build the portal. It leads to Earth, where you are from. Claiming Quintarria wasn't enough—his desire to conquer was not satiated—he looked to other worlds, and through building the portal, found yours. Now, he tries to make the portal function properly, to be stable enough for him to take his armies to Earth and take your world, too."

"So, we gotta get rid of that portal, huh, Don?" said Kevin. "Ain't that right, Marrinoff?"

"Yes, Kevin, that is absolutely right. That is the final step to your quest. You are to weaken his grasp on Quintarria by assisting taking back the major cities for the Elves, one of which you have claimed. Then, Lale and I will take back the Life Plant. Lastly, you must destroy the portal Serranti, at this very moment, works to make function," Marrinoff explained. "The Life Plant is encased by a black crystal tower Serranti built to channel its energy to the top of the tower, where he works on the portal."

"Well, let's go," said Amanda as their nest in the swamp came back into view.

"One more thing, then yes. I commend your attitude, Amanda. Action. Truly an Elven way of thinking. Asope is waiting for our attack on the Life Plant's three Dark Elf guardians after you reclaim Laranda. He and the half-Elves will take Pariss at that time."

"So, all we have to do is Laranda and then the portal. Right, Marrinoff?" said Kevin.

"That is exactly right, Kevin."

"Awesome. We gotta do this."

"You have the heart of a brave warrior, like Amanda."

"You have the stout mind of a bold fighter and diplomat, sir Marrinoff," Kevin said with a deep bow.

"What about Donny?" Amanda said. "He's a human baby, right? Not a brave and commendable warrior at all." She stuck her digital tongue out at Donny.

"Donny will have the hardest job of all as a human. He will be the one to undo Serranti."

"What do you mean?" Donny asked. He liked the idea that he was special in this game. He smiled in the basement, glad nobody could see.

"You will see. You must stay alive; it is your purpose. Now, on to Laranda."

"Wait," Amanda said. "Is there a Save Point fountain around here? I have to pee."

*

They hid low in a canoe to get into the swamp city of Laranda. It had no roads, only canals. All the carved stone structures of the low-built city were covered in heavy, dark green moss. The greenery all throughout the city was overgrown, unkempt.

Donny kept wondering about Marrinoff's comment that he must stay alive, but it wasn't long before they were seen by the Trolls on the riverbanks, and it was time to fight. Amanda, Donny, and Marrinoff had their hands full. Everything was ranged, with their firing from the canoe against the Trolls on the banks, and Kevin didn't like it one bit. He continually called out battle commands to the rest of them, which they ignored, frustrating him even more. "Fireball, foul pink-haired Troll on left, low HP—be bold, young Wizard!" and "Triple Shot, yon Elven maid of might—green-haired Troll, middle, defeat!" and then, "Aw, man, *come on!*" when one of them didn't do as told.

Marrinoff mainly used his bow and could kill many enemies at once, like Melarrine and Eln had been able to do. Donny loved Unholy Storm. Shadowy Wizard figures flew at enemies from his wand. He could attack many at once, too, but had to stay on top of his curing at the same time. It was a lot of work, and the experience points poured down on them like Marrinoff's Rain of End Times rained arrows down on the Trolls, and soon after, the Dark Elves from the city. It was the first time they'd fought a Dark Elf other than Neea.

For all Donny knew, they wiped out every Troll and Dark Elf in Laranda, much to Kevin's dismay, but Donny reminded him there was still the Chimera.

Yep, the city had to be empty of enemies except for the Chimera, thought Donny as they crossed through the overgrown city center to the Palace of Laranda. Not a Dark Elf or Troll was anywhere anymore.

The three of them were now Level 49. Donny loved how fast they leveled sacking cities. He thought Amanda had the stat theory right. His Strength was higher than before after using Unholy Storm so much, but his Purpose stat was really getting going. All those Cures. She had to be right.

Asope had said Marrinoff could explain Purpose's purpose better than he could, but they'd all been too bedazzled by the Watcher Elf to remember to ask about it. Donny made a mental note to bring it up after the Chimera.

"Inside," Marrinoff said, "in the entrance hall, we shall meet the Chimera. None go in the Palace of Laranda anymore, nor have they for a long, long time. It is the domain of the Chimera."

"We need a plan, then, right, Marrinoff?" Kevin said.

"We certainly do, Kevin, but we do not have time. We must go."

"We go? We just go?" said Donny. He didn't know anything about the Chimera, but he'd seen pictures of one or two on the covers of fantasy books he'd read. What would this one be like?

"Yes, dweeb. We go. Don't be a chicken," Amanda said.

"Yeah, Don. Don't be scared. I'll protect you," Kevin added.

Donny sighed as Kevin marched right to the huge wooden double doors of the Palace of Laranda, and instantly swung them open—

—and Kevin was flattened by the Chimera just as quickly as it blew from within the palace. There was no way to live through that, and Kevin certainly didn't.

Damnit! Donny thought, and quickly pulled up his Resurrect spell, bringing his friend back to life and armed with 190 fresh HP.

The Chimera was enormous. Donny didn't know how it had fit inside the palace, much less got through the doors. It did, indeed, have three ghastly heads—one, a brightly colored orange and black tiger head with glowing green eyes; another, a red-scaled dragon with black spikes and flames spewing from its snout; and a third that looked like an old image of Satan as a goat with horns on its head that looked made of gold. The Chimera's body was tan and furred, with giant, red, hard-veined wings and a long, thin, maroon scorpion tail. Pincher included.

Donny flicked his sparkling wand and Cured Kevin for 98HP. Kevin held up his ax and shield.

The Chimera spun on Donny, with its tiger head closest to Donny. It roared like a train in the dead of night, huge and toothy jaws opened, and the tiger head launched at Donny.

Tiger Bite took over a hundred HP off him.

Amanda threw knife after knife at the tiger head. Donny didn't know she could do that. He thought she had to throw them all at the same time. Huh. The tiger head ducked down and lunged at Amanda, but she dodged.

The only thing Kevin could think to do was assume his Savior mantle. The Chimera instantly became enraged and put the offending Dwarf at the center of its wrathful aim.

"Not a good idea!" Amanda cried. "You can't take its hit! It's frickin' Level 60, with 70 Strength!"

But it was too late to reconsider. Kevin was right smack-dab in the middle of danger, as usual, and that was the dragon head's jealously guarded domain. Its black, oily tongue flickered out, and blackish-red flames shot out of its maw toward him. Kevin blocked the Dragon Breath, deflecting most of the damage, but Donny knew his friend's health was too low already. He immediately Cured him, but wasn't sure that would be enough for another hit.

The damned thing had 1,500 Hit Points, Amanda knew and told them, and she did all she could, using her ability to Throw Knives at the Chimera. The monster took 124 HP damage and was stunned for three seconds, which wasn't much, but it was something.

Marrinoff decided then was the perfect time to show off. He held his great bow pointed at the sun, aimed carefully, yet swiftly, and shot it.

Sunrays melted down onto the Chimera with his Apocalypse move.

But this only served to whip the Chimera into a greater fury. It underwent a Rage Boost, its body glowing red, and Donny knew from reading the game chat log that its attacks would now do triple the damage as before.

"Shit, I was afraid that would happen," said Amanda.

Marrinoff aimed straight at the Chimera's face, squinted one eye almost shut, and let his silver arrow—Donny knew this move from the game log when they fought Trolls on the riverbanks. It was the Death Shot—it flew right into the monster's head. Donny didn't see how much damage Apocalypse did, but Death Shot caused 265 points of damage.

The Chimera turned its devil goat-head head to Marrinoff. In a flash, it snapped at him. Baphomet Bite took almost 500 points from the Elf, but Donny was able to Cure him. Then he had to do it again almost instantly.

Marinoff was anything but grateful, however, snapping at Donny, "*Do not Cure me again.*" He loosened another Death Shot at the Baphomet's head, but to no avail. This was just getting worse and worse, and even one as powerful as Marrinoff couldn't show Donny how they would pull this off.

Kevin had learned his lesson about attracting the thing's furious attention by becoming Savior, and so contented himself with executing a few simple Slices on the creature's clawed feet.

Donny watched as Amanda had to dig deep to think of how she could make a difference in this fight. None of her usual tricks were working against such a powerful enemy. Donny smiled under his 3D controller as Amanda cast Invisible.

She raced around the beast, under it, everywhere, firing Triple Shot after Triple Shot, doing massive damage throughout the chaos that ensued, and driving the Chimera insane with untold anger and frustration at its unseen attacker.

The Chimera eyed Donny with its one good head—the utterly terrifying tiger head and, almost mocking the young Wizard, performed a Tiger Bite that ripped out Kevin's chest even as the Dwarf tried in vain to raise his shield against the attack. But he couldn't live with his heart inside the monster's mouth, and died instantly.

Donny was able to Resurrect him one last time in a flash without a thought, and Kevin screamed in a fury of his own, "*No, wretched beast!* You shall not have my last breath! You *will* feel my Shield Bash!" and executed the highly damaging move, which hurt the Chimera so much that it fell right on top of him.

You idiot! Donny thought and used a levitate scroll drop to lift up the Chimera enough to slide out his injured friend.

Donny uses Unholy Storm. Chimera takes 203 damage.

Neat, Donny thought. All his Wizard ancestor ghosties usually hit a group of bad guys, but it looked like Unholy Storm spread its damage out or focused it all on one big hit like that.

The Chimera's scorpion tail flipped around, spiking into Donny with a Tail Bite, doing 167 damage. Donny Cured himself even as the hit came, but the Chimera wanted him dead, dead, dead now. He couldn't take another hit. All its heads had turned toward him, mouths open, and the tail was coming back for round two.

Chimera uses Four Bites on Donny.

Kevin Blocks Chimera, deflecting 506 damage. Donny takes 102 damage.

Donny was so close to biting it. He thanked Kevin in his mind.

Marrinoff got into that position again, the Apocalypse position, with his bow pointed at the sun… and then bam! Sunrays poured down on the Chimera, and it called out as it burned.

"Amanda, how is it not dying?" Donny called to her from across the palace yard. They were all spread out from the Chimera except for Kevin, who was in its face, not worried about dying again, which he would with one hit after that boost the Chimera gave itself.

"It has something called Take Light, and it looks like it's like my Regain."

"Very astute, Amanda," Marrinoff said as he drew back his bow again. "It is stronger than Regain, however."

Marrinoff uses Death Shot on Chimera. Chimera takes 287 damage.

The Chimera wasn't playing around anymore. It turned on Marrinoff so fast Donny didn't have time to wonder what move to take next. It slammed him with Four Bites, and all three of the Chimera's heads chomped down on Marrinoff, with the tail snapping at him, dealing the devastating blow. One more hit, and Marrinoff was gone. His HP was at 41.

Donny Cures Marrinoff.

Chimera Breathes in Donny's Cure. Chimera gains 198HP.

"It took my Cure!" Donny said.

The Chimera's tiger head swung at Marrinoff. Mouth snapped open. Down it went...

Kevin Blocks Chimera, deflecting 392 damage. Marrinoff takes 39 damage.

Kevin becomes Savior. Chimera is enraged at Kevin.

Donny tossed Cures at Kevin, and had to admit he was impressed with Kevin's sudden agility with his blocking skills, but had to get the attention off of Kevin. Amanda was now throwing knives from wherever she was, but the Chimera couldn't attack her. Desperate, Donny used Unholy Storm on the Chimera... and then looked at his chat log.

He'd done 506 damage. He'd never done that much damage. He looked up in the log. Amanda's knives were doing 300-350 a hit.

"Why are we suddenly hitting so hard?" Donny asked, breathless.

"Your Power of One. It weakens Purpose over the course of a fight gradually," Marrinoff explained quickly. He hunched on the ground, a golden bubble around him which Donny assumed shielded him from losing his two HP. Donny hadn't been able to get a Cure on him through it, either.

"Ohhh," Donny said. He hadn't figured that out, that Power of One worked over time.

"Stand back, young one. This foe is beyond you. No offense," Marinoff said to Amanda.

"None taken if you kill that damned thing," she shot back.

The great Watcher Elf stood slowly from his bubble and literally rolled up his gilded sleeves. He aimed his arrow at the sun, pulled back the bow almost to the breaking point, and roared, "Sear in my *Apocalypse*, foul demon!"

It sustained some damage. Some.

"Dammit, it won't freaking die!" Amanda said. Donny couldn't see her. She was still invisible to avoid taking damage.

Again, unexpectedly, the Chimera acted out of character for most monsters in this game. It turned on Kevin and swooped in a wide arc toward the Dwarf, who stood ready even though there was no way to really be ready for a giant Chimera with its sights on making an end of you. He crossed his axes in front of him and screamed, "Do your worst!"

Which, Donny could see, was exactly what it was going to do. What did he have to end this madness and kill this nigh-unkillable beast? Fireballs, magic scrolls, or even the most powerful spell he had used in this game, Unholy Storm, wouldn't be enough to take down this giant red killer lizard monster thing. It would have to be something as great as the realms themselves…

That was it! The spell would have to be something beyond the earthly realm, something absolutely *celestial*.

He had one scroll…but right at the top of it were three Xs that looked like they were made with human blood. With it, he would invoke Meteor Swarm, a spell so devastating that it would drain him of all power long enough that, if the Chimera survived, it could kill him by stepping on him. Also, rocks of fire would fall from the sky and vaporize anything within a 40-meter radius of its target—including his compatriots. "Get back, guys! You too, Marinoff!"

The Watcher Elf raised an eyebrow.

"Meteor Swarrrrm!!!" Donny used the scroll and squinted.

Marinoff jumped back so fast he almost flew. Kevin and Amanda didn't know exactly what Meteor Swarm was, but seeing the mighty Marinoff's reaction, they sprinted for cover as Donny unleashed the most powerful spell he had ever attempted.

The top of the dome of the open sky turned blood red, deeper than that of the Ruby Dragon, and in the center came castle-size boulders engulfed in yellow fire. The Chimera itself stopped and looked up.

It was still staring in a rage when hell fell down upon it and smashed it into broiling cinders of Chimera meat. The great, unearthly beast was no more.

"Yes!" Amanda yelped.

"You did it, Don! You killed the Chimera! You're such a badass," Kevin said as his body reanimated.

"I am impressed, young Wizard. You each have now reached Level 50! Now, make haste. Donny, you must get the Key of Laranda."

Donny ran to the monster's three heads, saw a chain on the tiger head, and reached into the thick fur around its neck, retrieving a gold key from singed fur. "I got it!" He held it up.

"Hurry," Amanda yelled. "I see Trolls coming from the swamp. They're onto us!"

Donny didn't look back as the Chimera's body faded. He dashed inside the palace, took the spiral stairs two at a time, and made it to the door of the Throne Room. Yes, there was a key hole.

"You actually listened to me," Amanda said from behind him. He glanced over his shoulder before sticking the key in. Amanda, Kevin, and Marrinoff were there, and coming up the stairs were about forty Trolls.

Donny jammed the key in the lock and turned it, and, without looking back again, ran inside past rows of tables full of rotted food to the throne. On it rested a black rock that looked like charcoal. He could hear the Trolls' snarfling breath and scraping toe claws as they chased him into the Throne Room, amidst Kevin's archaic battle cries.

He targeted the Troll Stone. Compared to the Chimera of doom, what were a bunch of knuckle-dragging Trolls? He barely broke a sweat casting a Fireball at their Stone.

Boom!

Suddenly, all the Trolls entering the Throne Room screamed at once. Donny whipped around. His other three fighting companions were right behind him, defending him.

The Trolls, all of them, had burst into flames. As quickly as they'd screamed, they were already dead.

Donny did it. They'd done it. They'd reclaimed Laranda for the Elves.

CHAPTER 9

"Marrinoff said to keep moving, so we'll just have to hope Asope figures out where we are to give us our Level 50 moves," said Kevin. "I think we should keep moving like Marrinoff said."

Amanda frowned, but kept walking through the thick, lush forest. "How will he? I mean, he teleports. I mean, how the hell would he know where we are?"

"He did the other times," Donny pointed out. As much as he wanted his Level 50 move, he just as much didn't feel like watching his sister flirt with a game character half-Elf. "We keep going. Right, Kevin?"

"Yeah, that's right, Don."

"Jesus. Okay, but we'll have to stop soon. I gotta pee real bad."

"All you do is pee, but I don't see where it all comes from," said Kevin. "I mean, you ain't drank nothing this whole time."

"I have a small bladder, dork."

"So do I, but I hold it. I gotta go, too. See? Holding it."

"Okay," Donny said. "You two go to the bathroom. I'll stay here, uh, playing the game? Waiting in the game? Can we do that?"

"I don't see why not," Amanda said. "Kevin looked at the clock that time. Nothing happened."

"Yeah, that's right," said Kevin. "Okay, hold the fort, Don. We'll be back. Amanda?"

"Okay, but I go first."

Donny wasn't surprised when their character forms disappeared after they'd taken off their goggles and headphones. He didn't question how Quest worked, but rather rationalized the whole experience. Yes, it made complete sense to him that if they took off their 3D controllers, they would simply disappear from the game world.

Donny listened to them climb the basement stairs while he looked around Nallia Forest. They were on their way to Serranti's crystal tower. They couldn't be far. No real fighting on the way. All the undead were companions of the Elves now, and the Trolls were dead. Any little monsters or Orcs that were lower level than them Kevin simply cut in half, no fuss. But no experience points. That was fine with Donny. He hated not having his Level 50 move, so it eased his anxiety about it that everything they came across to fight gave none. Kevin yelled, "Karate chop!" every time he hacked a bad guy down.

Marrinoff had told them Asope might be late. He had said now that the Elves had control of three of the Elven capitals again, Asope would be heavily involved in reclaiming Pariss with the other half-Elves of the city. Marrinoff himself had gone off somewhere to meet Lale, he told them, so they could prepare to take back the Life Plant while Donny's party fought Serranti to take down the portal.

Donny sat on the dry leaves of the forest and smiled, breaking up a leaf from the ground near him. What a great game. They were totally going to beat it, and soon. He was almost sad that it would be over, but what a ride.

Kevin had found some salvageable food on the banquet tables of the Palace of Laranda's Throne Room, but Donny wouldn't eat that stuff even though it was a game and he wouldn't really be eating it. "Rotund Relish" had grubs in it, and "Everlasting Cabbage" just sounded gnarly. Donny looked forward to seeing what they did—that is, if Kevin remembered to eat them for the fight.

The sun was setting in Quintarria, and the sky darkened. But Donny noticed it seemed to be darkening pretty fast and looked up.

His heart stopped.

There stood Melarrine, long, white hair blowing with the gentle breeze, and as it grew to almost night, Donny took in the figure next to him.

It was Serranti.

"I told you. Yes. I brought him right to you, Master," Melarrine said to Serranti, looking over at his "master" as though he worshiped him like a god. Waiting for his god's praise.

"Melarrine!" Donny yelled and hopped to his feet.

Serranti was even uglier than in Marrinoff's memory. His skin was just awful, with open sores oozing yellow pus all over his now-gray skin. He wore a black cloth robe adorned with solid silver spikes on his shoulders and down his back. He wore matching bracelets. How did he not scrape himself to death with those things?

Probably because he was death.

"Thank you very much, Melarrine. You have served me well. Your deeds will not be forgotten once I have taken back what is mine." Serranti's high-pitched voice cracked as though he had those awful sores in his throat, too. "Human, you should never have come here."

Donny thought fast but came up with nothing. Why did they have to go to the bathroom right then?

"I will make this easy. You know not what you have done, whom you have crossed," continued Serranti, slowly walking toward him. His feet made no sound on the dead, fallen leaves. He raised his left hand into the air, and it glowed sickly blue. Then, the light shot out at Donny.

The evil of all evils was trying to kill him! Crap! Crap, crap, crap!

He had no idea what to do, and hadn't yet died—but he would die, and soon, if he didn't figure out a plan. He saw the now-black sky above him as he fell on his back. He couldn't move. He yelled Amanda and Kevin's names, but they didn't come. They weren't done in the bathroom, couldn't hear him. What was he going to do?

"That was easy enough," said Serranti. "Now, Melarrine, for putting the tracking spell on the human and letting me know when the human was alone, I reward you with a place in my Crystal Tower. Burn his body. He will not fade, so this is how it must be done. Then, come to me and stay at my side." He turned away and walked out of Donny's view.

"Thank you, thank you, Master. I will always obey. I always have."

"You are a good half-Elf."

Donny heard a *whoosh*. Serranti must be able to teleport, too. Melarrine's disgusting face appeared over Donny. "So sorry Donny, but you are a fool if you think you can defeat one as powerful and purposeful as Serranti." He grinned wickedly and held out his staff. The stone in the top glowed bright white, and he extended his hand toward Donny.

Eln Gives Blood.

In one move, Donny popped back up, said "Thanks!" to Eln, and tried another scroll spell he'd never dared: Time Stop. It seemed so good he never wanted to use it and lose it.

He quickly used the scroll...

...and time indeed stopped. No one moved, not his friends, not Eln, not Melarrine.

He stepped up and punched the Wizard-Knight right in the jaw. He didn't fall, didn't move at all, until the spell wore off and Mellarrine went ass-over-tea-kettle onto the ground. He estimated that the traitor took 125 damage or so, but that hardly mattered.

Eln was stepping up now.

"Melarrine, you have been a very, very bad half-Elf." Eln's black form shot from the sky straight for Melarrine's throat, and placed upon him the deathly Eternal Kiss.

Mellarrine squealed until he could no longer make sound, and he fell over, dead.

"Holy crap!" Donny said. He could feel his eyeballs popping out of his head as though they couldn't see enough of this. Eln drank deeply from limp Melarrine's neck until the wicked, lying half-Elf faded. Eln had not only brought Donny back to life, but he'd also saved him from having his game body burned, and had exacted revenge on his betrayer. "Eln, thank you so much. I can't believe it. You... you saved me, and our quest."

Eln straightened up and spat some blood on the forest floor. "Disgusting. At least he had some Elf. Not all Dark Elf. Dark Elves are bitter, like eating spoiled meat for you, perhaps." He smiled at Donny. "I've been watching you between feedings. I must protect my way home."

"Of—of course, Eln. You definitely did." He grinned up at the towering vampire. "Thank you."

"Maybe your friend Kevin is right about me, you're thinking. Well, he is. You will take me home to Earth, and after hearing of you with the Chimera, I've no doubt it can be done. Not surprised about that disgusting," he spit again, made a face, "half-Elf, Melarrine. Filthy business. Serranti, as I said, works with allies of all kinds. Trust I am not one of them."

"Of course not."

"Now, Don, I'll let you in on a secret. You do not have to tell your companions this." He walked toward Donny like a cat prowling the yard at night. "I'll be with you until the end, and at the end, I expect my help to be rewarded in the manner you promised. You will not see me, most likely, but I will be there. I implore you to keep your side of the bargain you made when I defeated the Ruby Dragon for you."

"Yes, Eln. Of course, Eln. I wouldn't have it any other way." Donny was too excited. He couldn't wait for Amanda and Kevin to come back. He had to tell them everything that had happened, especially that Eln seemed to be their guardian angel. A dark guardian angel, but truly just that.

Eln bowed his head slightly. "Now, back to the shadows I go. Fight Serranti at night, please, and this night best of all. I so very much crave my Earth, my Earth life, and want it back as soon as possible. You can certainly do it."

"I will. We will, Eln. Thank you." Donny took a step back as Eln flew high into the dark sky and vanished.

He heard Amanda and Kevin coming down the basement stairs. Amanda called Kevin a goon for some reason, and then she said, "Donny, who are you talking to? Donny?"

"You gotta get back in here, guys. You won't believe what just happened."

CHAPTER 10

Asope met them as they hid in the foliage of Nallia Forest outside Serranti's crystal tower. He had told them that the half-Elves took back Pariss, which was why he'd been delayed in giving them their Level 50 abilities. "Many half-Elves were lost, but overall, we were victorious. Many more Dark Elves and Orcs perished, yet Kleemop, the Orc shaman guarding over the Orcs of Pariss, escaped with his life. He traveled to lower world to hide, and none but a shaman can reach lower world."

Amanda had gotten the move Straight Shot, which Asope told her with a grin would make her arrows go around bends—this move never missed. She had stuck out her chest, flipped her hair, and thanked him with a big, useless laugh.

Kevin got Hero, which Asope said gave him the option of taking someone's damage when they were hit. Kevin also puffed out his chest, but not to flirt. He couldn't wait to die for somebody.

Donny got the spell Cure All. Asope told him it would Cure his party members to full HP all at once. He was psyched.

Asope had said that he had a hard decision picking Donny's next move, but chose Heal All because, from rumors of the kids' fighting, Donny sure loved to Cure.

He told them Lale and Marrinoff were close by, and the kids should wait until the two Elves entered the crystal tower to take the

Life Plant before they themselves entering and going to the top of the tower to destroy the portal and end Serranti's reign.

Donny couldn't stand waiting. With Cure All, there was no way they'd lose. He'd simply use Cure All constantly. Right? No dying.

The tower was solid dark quartz crystal, and the base of it glowed a faint, deathly blue from the imprisoned Life Plant, while the top, five stories up, pulsed with flashes of lightning and an odd hue of black light.

"Hey, there's Marrinoff," whispered Kevin. "Over there, across from us in the woods. See?"

"Yeah," said Donny, spying Marrinoff, and then Lale's fiery frame across the crystal tower's glade. Where was Asope? Maybe, with Marrinoff's imposing stature and Lale's flamy self, Asope's figure was overpowered.

It was close to dawn in Earth time, and Amanda was hellbent on finishing the game by sunrise.

"Hello." It was a familiar voice behind them, one Donny hadn't heard since yesterday. He spun around.

Howlinowa stood behind them, cloaked as before, still not showing his face.

"Hey, Howlinowa!" said Kevin. "I didn't think we'd ever see you again."

"Shhh! You're so damn loud," Amanda scolded, and then looked at Howlinowa. "Uh, hi there," she whispered. "Can you keep it down?"

"They cannot hear me. Only those I wish to see and hear me may," he said, and leaned on a crooked wooden cane. "I have come because you are at the end of your quest. What happens next, here in Serranti's crystal tower, determines the fate of both Quintarria and Earth. Your party have the power to end a three thousand-year reign of terror, and stop one coming to your own world."

"We're gonna do it," Kevin bragged. "Don's got a plan. You know about his new spell?"

"I know."

"Okay." Kevin squatted down and gestured for Howlinowa to do the same.

"Idiot. He just said nobody but us can see him," Amanda said, also squatting low. Donny did the same.

"It's time when idiots win, Amanda," said Kevin.

"Shut up."

"Now," Howlinowa said, interrupting Kevin's not shutting up. "I am here to help you finish your quest."

"Purpose," Amanda said. "Are you going to tell us about Purpose? The stat? What does it mean to this game? We have to know that to beat it, I'm just sure."

Donny was glad she'd thought to bring it up. Again, he'd forgotten all about it.

"Yes, Purpose is the most determining stat in Quintarria. Serranti's Purpose is at 90. No, he is not a healer, but his Warlock spells are twisted with malevolent and self-indulgent Purpose. Donny, you are the key to stopping him. You are human. With Power of One, you bring his Purpose down, all the way to half that amount. None can do this but you."

"We have to fight him for a while, then," said Donny. "When we fought the Chimera, my Power of One was gradual. Marrinoff explained that."

"Yes, that is correct."

"Why didn't you just tell us that when we started the game?" Amanda asked.

"I did."

Silence.

"No, you didn't." Amanda couldn't help herself.

"I did."

Silence again.

"Fine, you told us," Amanda finally said. "Is that what you came here now to 'tell us' again?" She made air quotes.

"Yes."

"Why would you have to tell us again if you already told us?"

"Because people from Earth have bad memories." He bent over his cane, and turned his head toward them, his hood falling back off his head with a twitch of his neck. His face was a fleshless, black skull.

His open eye sockets seemed to watch all of them at once. Donny felt a chill creep over his skin. The lipless, fleshless mouth opened, black teeth shining in the moonlight. "I chose you three to do this, and you shall, as you said, Kevin."

"Oh, my God! What are you?" said Kevin.

"I just used Insight," Amanda said. "He does have all Level 0s, and no abilities. Yeah, what are you?" Her voice was hushed. Apparently, she'd finally been humbled by Howlinowa's ghastly face.

"I am the Game Host, no more, no less." The black teeth clacked together as he talked. Donny wondered how a skull had a voice, then tried to stop thinking about it. He both wanted to look away and couldn't stop gaping at him.

"O-okay, Game Host Howlinowa. Thanks man, you're, uh, the best. Yeah," Kevin stuttered out. "We got this, like I said. But any other help... yeah... would be appreciated."

"Serranti expects the attack to reclaim the Life Plant," he said, "but he thinks Donny is dead, and that you two," he pointed at Kevin and Amanda with a black, boney finger, "have not returned to Quintarria. His spy is dead, but Serranti is selfish, does not care, does not wonder why his spy has not yet joined him at his side. He focuses instead, on making the portal function. He craves escape; he knows the Elves will come and be successful. You three must deactivate the portal, and you must go through it to do that. Through it back to Earth."

"I can take my 3D controller off and be back on Earth," said Kevin. "See? I just slipped my goggles down a little and the cuckoo clock says it's six. That's in the morning. See? I did it again."

"Yes, but what I just told you is that to close the portal, you must destroy it from the inside."

"Oh. Wait, no. That's not what you said," argued Kevin, acting confused.

"Shut up, goon. It's how we beat the game," hissed Amanda as she whacked the back of his helmet.

"Stop it! Okay, okay. I get it."

"Now, you fight. Turn around."

Donny looked behind him at the crystal tower. The top pulsed black and white madly now, even as Lale, Marrinoff, and Asope crossed the glade and entered the tower from its ground-level crystal door.

"Yeah, we gotta go," said Donny, and he turned back to Howlinowa.

He was gone.

"Hey, where'd he go?" Kevin asked, not seeming to expect an answer.

"Do you talk just to hear your own voice, dweeb?" Amanda said.

"I talk because I'm explaining everything to you, because you might not understand. That's how dumb you are, Amanda."

"God." She sounded bored with everything.

"How do we get up there?" Donny asked as the bottom of the crystal tower lit up with battle, and sounds of outright war took over the still air. The three Elves must be fighting the three Dark Elves who had to be tending the Life Plant for Serranti, Donny thought.

"You fly."

Donny looked directly overhead, and saw Eln floating there.

"Eln, you have perfect timing," Donny said, and smiled up at him.

"Eln! Thanks for saving Don!" Kevin hollered over the noise of warfare coming from the bottom of the crystal tower.

"Of course. I have an extremely vested interest in how this turns out. We will fly now."

"What, all of us? Togeth—"

Without another word, Eln cast the spell of Flight.

They floated up in a triangle around Eln, who swooshed them up to the top of the crystal tower, and its radical light from the portal within was more lively than ever.

Serranti had to be activating the portal.

"Now, Earthlings, in you go."

"There's no window," Kevin said.

"Do you think I don't have this covered? Particles!" Eln pronounced, and the entire crew particulated into a fine mist. Donny felt his game body spread out around him as Amanda and Kevin seemed to disappear.

"Go, quickly, through the wall. Now." Eln sounded almost angry that they hadn't gone yet.

Donny pushed forward on his joystick... and zoomed right through the crystal tower's top level wall.

Inside, everything was dark except for Serranti's portal, which looked the same as when Marrinoff showed it to them, except the black-on-black of its spinning seemed dizzier, and the lightning sparks on its edges were straight-up lightning bolts shooting to the edges of the circular room, cracking them with each strike. Serranti stood before it, one deformed hand reaching out spindly fingers toward the dark center.

"Stop!" Donny yelled as he retook his form, landing perfectly on his feet.

Serranti spun to face him. "Human! How do you yet live?"

Amanda and Kevin took form on either side of Donny. "We have friends, unlike you," said Kevin.

"He had a friend," said Amanda, glaring at Serranti, "but he's dead as a doornail."

"Melarrine, dead?" His distorted, puss-filled face twisted in rage. "He was my grandson! How *dare* you!"

Serranti held up both arms, and they didn't look frail anymore. They looked more like metal pipes welded by a drunk in the night. The air swirled around him into a funnel, quickly taking shape of not air, but water.

"Shit," Amanda said. "He's casting Flood!" She must have seen Flood with Insight, and to Donny, she sounded scared.

A tidal wave washed over Kevin and Donny, but Donny couldn't see Amanda and didn't know if she was getting hit too. He spun around and around, and almost felt like he actually was drowning. In the flood, he spied Kevin swirling like a top a few feet away.

Serranti targeted him and moved to send him down a whirlpool to his incurable death.

Donny blocked the new spell with his very last loot magic scroll, and shot it back at the Dark Elf. Serranti's black robes, soaked, floated around him, then whipped like nightmares. Far from being defeated by this, he seemed to generate wind energy from the reflected spell. He actually snarled and moved again to end the young Wizard.

"He's really freaking after you, Donny," Amanda said from nowhere, as she had turned Invisible. She'd been doing her new shoot-from-anywhere-and-never-miss shot. Enjoying it even in the midst of deadly chaos, too.

Donny screamed—really screamed—as Serranti spun a spiral of wind right into his eyes. Donny had suffered a Dazzle spell; he couldn't move his game body or access his menu. He wrestled his joystick madly, but nothing happened.

He was going to die. What happened if he died here... really died? He didn't want to find out, but Serranti had built the wet storm around him again, ready for another Flood, and then let it all loose.

But somehow, incredibly, the wall of water stopped in place. Kevin had used Block, deflecting an amount of damage that would have decimated Donny. Wow, Kevin thought fast! Donny nearly passed out from relief.

Serranti threw Donny's favored spell, Fireball, and Donny knew darned well that Fireball would hit him with enough damage to send him into the beyond.

"I'm gonna die!" Donny cried out. "I can't die!"

"You won't die," Amanda yelled. "Not while I have good ole Straight Shot."

Serranti stumbled backwards at the hit from Amanda, sustaining 356 points of serious damage.

"Your Power of One, it's doing its thing!" said Kevin.

Serranti let out a howl.

Suddenly, Donny had control of himself again, and his menu reappeared. He immediately healed the party. But he saw something and shouted, "Wait!"

"What?" Amanda called out. The portal spun like a wild, dark Ferris wheel out of control and on super-high speed.

"We have to go through, look. Now!" Donny said.

Serranti also turned. His wicked mouth turned up around his flat, fat nose.

"Before he does. Come on!"

He hoped Amanda followed, but he couldn't be sure. Kevin slapped Serranti with a Slice, then ran with Donny toward the portal. Donny was impressed with how Kevin became such an amazing warrior at the last minute. He really protected them all, and as Serranti tried to jump through the black portal first, Amanda used Throw Knives to shave off more than 600 HP, and stun him long enough to stop him in his tracks.

"Yeah!" Donny yelled, and jumped into blackness itself. Kevin was right next to him, and Amanda became visible as she crossed over on Donny's other side. Donny spun around in the nothingness of the portal. "Eln!" he cried out. "Eln, come on!"

He saw a black figure zoom by and hoped it was Eln.

He looked around him. On one side, he saw Serranti, stunned, with a malevolent expression, and on the other side was his basement. He saw the three of them sitting on the floor wildly wrenching their joysticks this way and that.

He had to do something. His most powerful move. He called up the Wizard ancestors, and one of the ghostly figures actually looked back at him and grinned.

Donny knew Unholy Storm would work against Serranti, but he had no idea if it could do anything to shut the Infinity Portal. So he went for it. "Unholy Storm!"

Serranti got pulverized, eaten alive by ghostly ancient Wizard ghosts… and the Infinity Portal collapsed.

Donny got really, really dizzy, because everything spun around like he was on the Zipper at the fair. He heard Kevin and Amanda laughing, and then heard the loud, crashing sound of breaking glass, a lot of it.

He ripped off his goggles and headphones and looked at the basement window set high near the ceiling. The glass had just been broken, and Brian Boyd was dropping himself down to the carpet.

Amanda and Kevin had also torn off their 3D controllers, and Amanda was already in action. She pulled her switchblade out of her jeans' pocket. "What the shit? Freak!"

Kevin quickly looked around, and then picked up the Atari itself, holding it, cables and all, like a shield.

Duff and Ernie came through the window at the same time, right behind Brian, who stood straight and reached up for Duff's baseball bat. "You dumb whore, you don't even know how to use that thing."

"You better freaking believe I know how to use it, bitch." She ran at him just as Kevin did, but Ernie grabbed Kevin under his arms before he could reach Brian. Ernie threw him to the ground, but he popped back up and swung the Atari at Ernie's head.

Down Ernie went.

"That's what you get, dark, smelly demon!" Kevin yelled.

Amanda and Brian were going toe-to-toe in circles, bat and knife swinging at empty air.

Duff came straight for Donny.

Donny thought fast, and yanked a pair of goggles with their cables off of the Atari Kevin now threw at the back of Ernie's fallen head. They came free easily, and Donny grasped tightly to the end of the loose wires.

He swung the goggles in an arc to where they twisted around Duff's neck. The bully grabbed his throat, but it was too late. Donny pulled, and down Duff went, right next to Ernie.

"You goddamn assholes!" Brian yelled, and the bat went straight for Amanda's head.

Amanda ducked expertly, and threw the switchblade at Brian's gut as she did.

It landed, and a spot of red spread across his belly from under his shirt. He looked down, ripped the knife out, and glared up at Amanda. "I have it now." He dropped the bat and slowly walked toward Amanda with a demented grin, like he was about to really enjoy cutting Amanda up.

Donny slid on the carpet and grabbed the bat by the handle, standing up behind Brian just as he slashed at Amanda. Donny lifted the bat up over his head, closed his eyes, and screamed, "You goddamn bully! Leave my sister alone!" He brought the bat down on Brian's head.

Down he went, and dark red rushed from the wound Donny delivered. Brian landed on the floor on his belly and flipped around. Man, was he bloody. Kevin continually brought the Atari down on both Duff and Ernie's heads, keeping them away while Donny and Amanda taught Brian a lesson.

A lesson about how he wasn't going to mess with their family anymore.

Amanda kicked Brian in his switchblade wound over and over, keeping him down, yet still he struggled against her.

Donny slowly walked over to him, put both feet on either side of his head, and put the baseball bat against his nose. Brian stopped trying to get Amanda, and stared up at Donny, eyes wide with shock.

"Don't get up, Brian," Donny warned. It was so, so tempting to just knock his stupid head off.

"Donny, don't," Amanda said. She sounded scared.

Donny kept his eyes on Brian's. "You will never mess with me, Kevin, or Amanda ever again. Right?"

Brian started crying. The switchblade fell out of his hand, and Amanda grabbed it.

"I didn't hear you," Donny said. "You will never, ever mess with us again. Say it!"

He blubbered now, and covered his eyes with his arms. "Please, please stop!"

Donny stepped away and planted the bat in the kid's chest. He looked at Kevin holding the Atari high in the air, and then at Amanda, now on the floor after a crafty foot grab by Brian. "Now what?" he said.

"You feed," said a voice from the dark, open closet, and then they heard cackling. A black figure darted out of the window.

"Eln?" Kevin whispered.

Just then, sunlight peeked through to the basement, and Killer and the rest of Amanda's bandmates climbed inside from the broken window. "'Manda? We were in front, and they got around us," Killer said.

"Damn," said the hairless singer. "You three kicked some ass! All right!"

So that's what Amanda had been doing with Killer that night. She had been making a plan against the three bullies in case something like this happened. Might have started as something else, typical stuff she always had to do, but the phone call had freaked her out.

"Killer," Donny said. "Can you three carry these pieces of crap out of our house?"

"Oh, hell yeah, we can."

*

Donny was exhausted. He wasn't the only one. He had been amazed that Amanda could drive to downtown Chattanooga after being awake for over twenty-four hours. She was determined to be the ones who beat Quest the fastest.

"The old guy will be shocked as shit to see us, right?" Amanda said as they walked down the cracked, quiet Sunday sidewalk toward Royee's shop.

"No kidding," Kevin said. "Especially that we're giving the game back. Who in their right minds would give Quest back? It really is the best game ever made."

"Well, we did try it again," Donny reminded him. "It didn't work. That means we beat it, right, Amanda?"

"That's what we're gonna find out," she said.

They reached Royee's shop and Kevin yanked the glass door open. They went inside the dark, musty, cluttered shop. As expected, nobody was inside.

"Hello? Old guy?" Amanda called out. "You in here? Got your tealight?"

"Don't call him old guy," chided Kevin.

"What, you hit a couple thugs on the head and think you can tell me what to do?"

"Shh," Donny told them as a gentle light came toward them from the back of the shop. "Royee?" he said. "Is that you?"

He came into view. He wore the same brown bathrobe, but was barefoot. And yes, Donny saw he carried a tealight in his palm. "Hello, yes? Oh! It's you three. I didn't expect you so soon." He reached them and smiled. "Well, what have we here?"

"We want to know if we beat the damn game," Amanda said.

"Amanda!" Donny said. "Be quiet!"

"Don't tell me to shut up, or I'll shut you up for good."

"If you beat... the game... hmmm." He looked over them curiously. "Done already?"

"We closed the portal, but had to stop playing right then and there because, well, stuff happened," explained Kevin.

"Closed the portal. Well, well. That is all very good. I'd say, then, that if you closed the portal, you beat the game." He smiled and set the tealight on the dragon book table. "Were you pleased with the dragons, young man?" he asked Donny.

"Yeah. They were so cool," he said, and smiled at Royee. "You're saying we did beat it? Because we tried to make it work again, but it didn't."

"Uh, I hit a couple deadbeats over the head with the Atari, and the game was still in it, so we didn't know," Kevin said.

"Do we get anything for beating it?" Amanda said, hand on hip, head cocked to the side. She had dropped all the cables, goggles, headphones and the microphone on the table.

Royee's eyebrows shot up. "Well, I do think you'd have the eternal gratitude of the Elves."

"Yeah, but how do we know that?" Amanda persisted.

"Let me have a look at the game cartridge," Royee said, holding his hand out.

Donny gave him the game, back in its box. "Here you go."

He examined the outside of the box from all angles. "Yes, yes. This game has been completed. Very good job, children, and so fast!"

"Did we beat the record?" Amanda asked. She sounded hopeful to Donny.

"I don't know anyone else who has beaten it, so I do believe you're the record holders, why, yes!" He sounded delighted. "You liked my invention?"

"Liked it? It's the best game, I mean, the absolute best game ever made," Kevin said. "And we are the first people to beat it?"

"That is what I said, isn't it?"

"Yeah," Amanda told him. "That's what you said."

"Why then, it must be the truth. I wouldn't have said it if it weren't." He tucked the game box into his robe's pocket. "Because you returned the rental so very early—my gosh, it's only been a day!— I will grant you a reward based on your merit. I happened to get a copy of the Pac in yesterday afternoon. You just missed my delivery boy. I will give it to you."

"The Pac?" Donny said, his heart rate shooting up. "You mean, Pac-Man? You got Pac-Man?"

"Oh, I'm so very sorry. Yes, that is what I meant. The Pac-Man."

"It's just Pac-Man, dude," Amanda said.

"That's what I said, young lady. Listen…" He leaned down and looked her deep in the eyes. "Listen with your ears." He gently rapped his knuckles on Amanda's head and smiled.

All three of them were dead quiet, staring at Royee.

"Here, I have it in my other pocket. You, you paid last time. Here is the Pac-Man." He pulled the game that started it all out of his robe pocket and handed it to Donny, who took it with numb hands. "Thank you for trying out my game and taking such good care of it. I trust it'll be a hit when I put it on the market? Yes?"

"Uh, yeah!" Kevin said. "Are you kidding me?"

"Thank you for the compliment. That is what that was, am I correct?"

"Yeah. Yeah, Royee, it was," Donny told him. "And thanks for Pac-Man. And for the rental. And for… everything."

"Good, good! So glad for someone to be grateful to me. Nobody is grateful to an old man who collects what some call junk." He winked at Donny. "Off you go now, off to play more games. That's what all young people are good at. Playing games." He leaned back on his heels, looking extremely pleased with himself.

They turned and left the shop, walking quietly back the way they'd come.

"That was freaking weird," said Amanda. "Like, did he see us play?"

"It sure as shit seemed like it. And, hey. Was that really Eln when those jerks took over the basement? I mean, when we took over them?" Kevin asked.

"I don't know," Donny said. "It sure as shit seemed like it."

"Donny, shut up! Don't talk like that. God, Kevin, you're a terrible influence," Amanda said. "But, yeah. If that was actually somehow Eln, then maybe…"

"Maybe what?" Donny asked.

"Maybe that Royee… maybe he's Howlinowa?" she said.

"I didn't think of that," Kevin said. "You know, that kinda makes total sense."

"It does?" Donny asked. He stopped walking. The other two did as well.

Donny looked back at Royee's shop down the road. He squinted, and then shielded his eyes against the morning sun. "Where is it?"

Amanda and Kevin also looked back. "I don't see it," Kevin said. "Hey, where'd it go?"

"Well, I'll be damned," said Amanda.

Where Royee's shop had been just moments ago, where they'd been inside and talking to the odd Royee and had gotten Pac-Man—and Quest—now stood a black storefront. Donny squinted harder, trying to read the narrow sign above the door. It had a martini glass that suddenly lit up in neon green.

"Guys, can you read that? Does it say what I think it says?" Donny asked, heart pounding.

"Yeah. It sure as shit does, Don," Kevin replied.

The sign over the shop they'd just been in that no longer existed read, "The Portal."

Donny smiled at Kevin and Amanda. "Go figure."

133

THE END